FORTUITY

Fortuity Duet #1

ROCHELLE PAIGE

Edited by Ellie McLove (Gray Ink) & Manda Lee

Cover designed by LJ Anderson, Mayhem Cover Creations

Photographer: Sara Eirew Photography

Models: Daniel Rengering and Pamela Tremblay Mcallen

A Note From The Author

My decision to write romance novels was heavily influenced by my mom—the person who's responsible for me falling in love with them. I was dealing with some radical life changes, as well as helping my mom with the eleven-month process it took to get her placed on the transplant list. Reading became my escape more than ever, and that's when I discovered indie authors.

Writing had always been a dream of mine, so I started looking into what self-publishing was all about. When I mentioned it to my mom, she was excited about something for the first time in too long. With the fear that the call from the transplant team would never come hanging over our heads, we made a deal—I'd publish within a year and she would do her best to hold on to hope and stay as healthy as possible while we waited for the call. We were extremely lucky it came only a couple of months later.

I wrote part of *Sucked Into Love* from her hospital room and kept my side of the deal when I published *Push the Envelope* about nine months later. Without the desperation I felt over my mom's health and that random conversation about indie publishing which led to our deal, I don't know that I ever would have found the courage to fulfill my dream.

A few months later, the idea for Fortuity hit me. It's a story close to my heart because the heroine is a transplant patient. Fortuity has been building in my head for four years, and I'm so excited to share it with everyone.

Thank you for coming on this journey with me,
Rochelle Paige

The only kinds of luck I knew were bad and worse...until my life hung in the balance. I finally caught a break in the form of a second chance.
I vowed not to let it go to waste.
To make a difference.

But I didn't start really living until I met him.
Dillon Montgomery.
My complete opposite—except for our matching tortured souls.

I couldn't resist him for long.
How could I when his smallest touch made my heart race?
When it felt like we were destined to be together?

But sometimes luck and sorrow are intertwined...

Fortuity is the first part of Faith and Dillon's story, which will be completed in *Serenity*.

Prologue

FAITH

To say I had a difficult childhood was a major understatement. Being raised by an eighteen-year-old mom who had no idea who my father was came with certain complications. The kind that meant she was always pissed at me because it cost so much money to raise a kid, and she blamed me for not being able to go out and have fun all the time like her friends were doing. Her frustration quickly turned into bitterness; which led her down the path of destruction. Hers—and mine if she had her way and was able to take me along for the ride.

Once I was in Kindergarten, she was leaving me home alone for a couple of hours at a time when she wanted to go out with friends. When third grade rolled around, she had moved away from drinks with friends to meeting up with her drug dealer. One year later, it was overnight motel stays for "dates" she went on with "uncles" I knew I didn't have. As her need for drugs grew, she stopped checking in to a motel and started bringing them home instead.

By home, I meant the one-bedroom apartment she rented for us. Whenever she had a visitor, I needed to make myself scarce and there weren't many places to go. When I was in the fifth grade, I started using the laundry room in the basement as my safe haven. I'd drag my homework down there, along with a blanket and a pillow in a laundry bin. If I fell asleep in the corner where the sink was, I could squeeze part-way under it so nobody would see me unless they were specifically looking for me. I'd seen enough in my young life to be scared something bad could happen to me in the middle of the night, but I never considered the danger my mom was in. Not until when I was twelve and returned to our apartment one night only to find her naked body sprawled on the floor with vomit surrounding it.

"Mom!" I screamed as I shook her still form and tried to wake her up. When the chilliness of her skin registered in my brain, I realized she wasn't just passed out and something was seriously wrong. I ran to my room and grabbed blankets to toss over her body to try and warm her up. Then I dug through her purse for her cell phone and called 9-1-1. I was frantic as I explained what was happening, and the operator stayed on the line until an ambulance and the police arrived.

The paramedics didn't spend a lot of time working over my mom's body before they loaded her onto a stretcher and carried her down to the waiting ambulance. By this time, I was sobbing uncontrollably and the policeman was trying to calm me down and ask some questions. Fear of the unknown kept me silent because as horrible as my mom was, at least I knew what to expect with her. I didn't know who my father was and there wasn't anyone else I could call to take me in if she was going to be in the hospital for long. I didn't know what the police would do when they found out I was on my own, and it terrified me.

"She's in no condition to answer now," his female partner said. "We better call CPS and have someone meet us at the hospital."

He glanced at me before nodding. "Go ahead and get changed, sweetie. We'll make sure we take you to your mom."

I walked into the bedroom I shared with her

and started to shut the door for some privacy, but then their conversation drifted towards me. With the door open a crack, I leaned as close to it as I could get without making any noise so I could listen to what they were saying.

"When we call CPS we better tell them to send someone to meet us at the hospital," the policeman said.

"I know," his partner agreed.

"Did you see that shit?" he hissed.

"Yeah. Hopefully it's not too late for CPS to get her some help before she winds up just like her mom."

I wanted to run back into the living room and yell at him for daring to suggest that I would turn out anything like the woman who had given birth to me. My life might be crap, but that didn't mean I planned to eat shit for the rest of my life. But I resisted the temptation because I knew it wouldn't do any good. There wasn't anything I could say or do to change their minds.

I wasn't in control of much in my life, but I'd learned to focus on the few things I was because it made me feel like I was organizing the chaos a little bit. For the moment, all I could do was throw some stuff into my backpack so I had things to do while I was at the hospital with my mom. After checking to make sure I had everything I needed to do my homework, I grabbed a couple of books that I had borrowed from the school library and a change of clothes.

"I'm ready," I said as I walked down the hall, making sure they stopped talking about me and my sucky life before I made it into the room.

Being hustled into the back seat of the squad car parked at the curb in front of my building wasn't one of the best moments of my life. I felt like everyone was staring at me and thought I'd done something illegal. There was an awkward silence as we drove to the hospital. The guy cop was driving, and his gaze kept drifting back to where I sat brooding with my arms crossed protectively around my body. I was still pissed about what I'd heard him say and figured my hostility must have been shining through.

When we got to the hospital, the cops handed me off to a caseworker from Children's Protective Services. She asked me a ton of questions before she sat me down in the waiting room to go in search of someone who could let us know what was going on with my mom. She wasn't alone when she returned. There was a doctor with her, and both of them had serious expressions on their faces as they walked over to where I was sitting. After the caseworker sat down next to me, she took my hand in hers and squeezed. I knew the news wasn't going to be good before the doctor said a word.

"You're Faith?" he asked. I nodded in response, fear making my throat swell up so I couldn't speak. "I'm sorry to tell you that your mom didn't make it."

He said more after that, but I couldn't hear him over the buzzing sound in my ears. When I noticed his lips had stopped moving, I cleared my throat. "She's dead?" I asked disbelievingly.

"Yes, she was already gone when the paramedics arrived," he confirmed before looking at the caseworker. She nodded her head, and it must have been a signal to let him know it was okay for him to leave because he got up and walked away.

Once we were alone, the caseworker turned in her seat to stare into my eyes. "I'm so sorry for your loss," she began. "I bet you're probably scared right now, but I'm here to help. You're not alone. I'll make sure you have somewhere safe to go where you'll be taken care of while I work with the police to find family who can take you in."

I nodded to let her know I understood what she was saying, but I was too stunned to think about how to react right now. After she was done talking with some of the hospital staff, it was time to go.

Getting into the car with her, I felt like my life had hit rock bottom. I was only twelve and hadn't even hit puberty yet, but I'd already learned the world could be a cruel place when there wasn't anyone in it who cared if you lived or died.

Chapter One

FAITH

Five Years Later

Miss Stevens, the caseworker I met the day my mom died, tried her best to find family members who were willing to take me in, but there just wasn't much information for her to work with. My mom hadn't listed anyone as my father on my birth certificate, confirming what she'd told me growing up; she just didn't know for sure. That left me with only one option...the grandparents I had never met because they kicked my mom out of their house when they found out she was pregnant with me. It wasn't a surprise when they refused to take me into their home even though I had nowhere else to go. They'd washed their hands of me before I was born and had no desire to change their minds twelve years later.

I didn't have high expectations of other people, and my outlook served me well in the foster system. The kids who were soft had it the hardest because the transition was rougher for them. The absolute worst were the ones whose entire world had changed in the blink of an eye. The parents who had loved them were gone, and nobody was left to take them in, so they were tossed into the system with us throw-away kids. They weren't just soft, they were sad. Unfortunately, there wasn't anyone around to give a damn or help them adjust to life without their family so they had to figure it out for themselves.

The only constant in my life was Miss Stevens. Even when they tried to transfer me over to someone else, she insisted on keeping me as one of her "kids" as she liked to call us. She was always on my case about giving my foster parents a chance. "They're good people who just want to help you," she would say any time I got kicked out of one and sent to another, usually because I kept to myself so much it made people wonder if I had a personality disorder or something.

Maybe there really were good foster parents out there who did it for the love of kids, but I hadn't been lucky enough to meet any of them yet. And honestly, as nice as she was, what did she know about it anyway? In my experience, foster parents put on a good show when one of our caseworkers did a visit, but it was just temporary. Once it was over, we were back to our regular programming of disinterest and sometimes flat-out neglect.

It was the latter of the two which landed me in the hospital. When I first got sick, I thought it was just a sore throat and didn't worry much about it. By the time I could barely swallow and complained to my foster mother about it, her *real* child was sick too. Of course, she took him to the doctor right away and didn't even think that maybe I should go along since I'd been the first to catch whatever was starting to spread through the house. The doctor diagnosed him with strep throat; a highly contagious disease that any reasonable person would guess to also be the cause of my illness since our symptoms were identical. But since I was the brat who had infected her precious boy, my foster mother wasn't in a hurry to seek medical help for me. Almost a week later, when two of the other foster children got sick, she finally bothered to take me to an urgent care clinic. But the damage had already been done.

About a week later, I started having weird symptoms. It began with some swelling in my feet and I figured it was just from the insanely hot weather we were having. Then it moved to my belly, which could easily be blamed on my period since it was supposed to start soon. When my face started looking puffy, I finally wondered what might be wrong with me. An online search at the school library gave me a huge list of things that could be the cause of the swelling. Anything from my period to all the salty food my foster mother fed us. Deciding either of those were the most likely culprit, I told myself not to worry too much about it.

When my fingers, wrists, and elbows started to ache, I figured it was from the swelling. Then my pee turned an odd color, but I thought it was probably from some of the candy I had eaten at lunch when a classmate shared it with me. But the next morning, when I found blood on the toilet paper after I went to the bathroom, I couldn't explain it away. My period hadn't started yet so it was enough to freak me the hell out. I didn't trust my foster mother enough to take me to see a good doctor, and I was scared that maybe I was dying or something.

So I called Miss Stevens to ask for her help. It was the first time I'd ever reached out to her, and I think she was too stunned to do anything but agree to take me.

I met her at the curb when she came to pick me up because I didn't want anyone to ask questions about what was going on. Offering her a weak smile, I climbed into the car and quickly buckled up so we could get out of there before one of the other kids saw me. "Thanks," I whispered.

"You're welcome," she replied before an awkward silence filled the vehicle. She tried to strike up a conversation a few minutes later, but I was even more uncommunicative than usual. I was less than a year away from aging out of the system and didn't know what would happen to me if I was really sick.

Although it was only half an hour later, I felt like I'd waited hours before I was sitting across from the doctor and he was doing the physical examination. "I'll need to run some tests to make sure, but I think it's post-streptococcal glomerulonephritis," he said when he was finished. "It's a kidney disorder that sometimes occurs after infection with certain strains of Streptococcus bacteria."

"Like the strep throat I had a couple of weeks ago?" I asked.

Instead of answering right away, he clicked the mouse on his laptop a couple times and peered at the monitor. "I don't see anything in your chart about strep. Were you treated for it here?"

Sneaking a glance at Miss Stevens, I knew she was going to be angry I hadn't talked to her about this sooner. "No, my foster mom took me to the urgent care clinic, along with a couple of the other kids who had it too."

"I'll give them a call to get your records transferred over here. It's pretty rare for a case of strep that's been treated in someone your age to cause post-strep GM."

"Maybe we should have the other kids brought in to be checked over too," Miss Stevens suggested. "Since all of you caught it at the same time, they might be at risk too."

"I had it longer than everyone else," I whispered.

"How much longer?" the doctor asked.

Miss Stevens leaned over and took my hand in hers when I hesitated. "Faith, when did you get sick?"

"Maybe a week and a half before we went to the clinic," I answered softly.

She gasped at my response and turned to the

doctor. "Could the delay in her care be responsible for her being ill now?"

"Yes," he confirmed. "Letting strep go untreated can lead to further complications."

"Oh, Faith," she sighed. "I'm so sorry."

"It's okay," I reassured her. "You didn't know."

"But your foster mom did, didn't she?" she asked.

"Yeah," I admitted. "I got sick before Adam did."

"Did she get medical care for him right away?"

I looked down at my hands as I twisted them together in my lap. "Yes."

"Oh my goodness," she breathed. "Are you telling me your foster mother knew you were sick with the same symptoms as her son, ignored your illness even though she took him to the doctor, and then bothered to get you treatment only when the other kids came down with it too?"

In the face of her mounting anger, I just nodded my head. At my confirmation, she jumped out of her chair and began to pace the room. The doctor and I watched her for a moment before he interrupted her as she mumbled under her breath.

"I know there's a lot going on here, but we need to discuss Faith's medical needs sooner rather than later."

"What kind of medical needs?" I asked as Miss Stevens came to sit beside me again.

"I'd like to run some blood work to look for the antibodies to a substance produced by the bacterium that caused your bout of strep throat, check some of your levels, and do a urinalysis," he explained.

"Okay," I replied since that didn't sound too bad even though I didn't understand it all.

"You'll also need a couple of medications. An antibiotic to make sure we get all the infection out of your system, and I want to put you on a diuretic to help with the edema as well as a blood pressure medication since yours is high," he continued.

"Oh," I sighed. That sounded like a lot of different pills for me to keep track of.

"I'll make sure she gets the prescriptions filled and we have a plan in place to make sure she gets anything else she needs," Miss Stevens said. "Is there anything else we need to do?"

"Limit her salt intake and call me immediately if she has decreased urine output or any new symptoms develop."

Although my head was spinning, I didn't miss the mention of new symptoms. "Like what?"

"At this point, I want you to call me with anything unusual," he answered vaguely. "And I have to admit that I'm leaning towards hospitalizing her."

"Hospitalizing me?" I repeated.

"Usually post-strep GM can be cleared up in several weeks to a few months," he clarified. "But that's only if you receive the proper care for it. Considering the circumstances that brought you here today, I have some serious concerns about the type of support you'll receive at home."

"I've been taking care of myself for a long time, Doc," I joked weakly.

"I don't want to scare you any more than you already are, but you need to fully understand your condition," he said, taking a deep breath before looking at me with resignation in his eyes. "In a small number of patients, post-strep GM may get worse and lead to chronic kidney failure. Sometimes it can progress to end-stage kidney disease, which would require dialysis and a kidney transplant."

I'd spent years convinced I lived without hope. It took hearing those words to understand I wasn't as hopeless as I thought I had been. Or at least I hadn't been. Until that very moment, I was more similar to other teenagers than I ever would have admitted in that I thought I would have a long and fairly healthy life. I didn't smoke, drink, or do drugs —not after the way I had watched my mom destroy herself. Apparently, none of that mattered because a common childhood illness that could be easily treated with antibiotics had managed to become a possible death sentence for me.

In the following weeks, I discovered how low I could fall as my condition didn't improve. It didn't matter that Miss Stevens had all the kids pulled from the foster home where I had been staying or that she finally found one of the few nice ones for me to go to with a foster mother who really acted like a mom and treated me as though I was her own. She cared for me as the swelling got worse, my blood pressure shot through the roof, and my appetite disappeared.

When the time came for me to be admitted to the hospital, she visited almost daily for the first few weeks until there was another foster child who needed her to be home so she could properly care for them. Saying goodbye to her was one of the hardest things I had ever done because I'd come to care for her. It was impossible not to when she'd shown me such compassion, but I knew there were others who needed her more than I did since I had nurses and personal care attendants watching over me around the clock.

Kids came and went through the pediatric unit. Some of them even tried to befriend me before I got a reputation for being a loner. But with everything going on, I was even more closed off than usual. Trying to focus on anything but how sick I had gotten, I threw myself into my online courses in the hope that I'd be able to keep up with my studies so that I wouldn't have to repeat my senior year. As my condition continued to worsen, I worked even harder on my classes because I was suddenly obsessed with the idea that I wanted to at least graduate high school before I died.

They monitored everything about me on a regular basis, and I felt like studying was the only thing over which I had control right now. I couldn't eat what or how much I wanted because the doctors wanted to reduce the buildup of toxins that my kidneys would normally remove. My fluid intake was closely monitored so that I only drank the same amount I could pee. They brought me pills and took my vitals around the clock. But study time? That was all me. I could even turn on the laptop they'd provided and read to my heart's content. Nobody ever tried to tell me I couldn't...probably because they all knew I was on my way towards death's door.

When they first put me on dialysis, I felt better and started to think I could beat this thing. It was only supposed to be used for the short-term, but I was one of the unlucky ones because my kidney damage was so great that they thought dialysis may be permanently needed. That's when they started talking about a transplant. If I had any family who gave a damn, they would have tried to do a live donation. My rare blood type made me a difficult match, and being a foster kid only complicated it further.

I became obsessed with making the UNOS waiting list, even though there wasn't a damn thing I could do to influence their decision to list me. Or to put me high enough up that I even had a remote chance of getting the kidney I so desperately needed. When the day finally came and I was told I made the list, it hit me. In order for me to live, someone else must first die.

Although a part of me celebrated the fact that my chances of survival had at least slightly improved that day, I felt morbid. It was like I was wishing death upon another person. As though I was hoping to swap fates with them, even though I'd never want anyone else to have the crap luck I'd lived with all my life.

Then it was just a waiting game, watching my place on the list rise and fall depending on the results of my newest labs. Each of us were ranked by UNOS using a point system. It also took a number of other factors into consideration, including the degree of match between us and the donor and the length of time we had been on the waiting list. My place never went high enough for me to get my hopes up, though. The doctors knew I was a bad bet since I had no support system in place to help me after the transplant, and so did I.

The dialysis continued, but I knew I was getting worse and the day was drawing closer when I was going to run out of options. It was painfully obvious to everyone that I was starting to accept my fate, starting to believe the call would never come. Not for me. That's when the nurses started up the faith jokes—to try and raise my spirits and get me focused on staying as healthy as I could while I waited. And waited. And waited some more.

During all that time, I knuckled down and plowed through my school work like it was the one thing that could save my life. Although I knew I wasn't going to be able to return to school to finish my senior year, I wasn't willing to completely give up until I finished all my courses and knew I had accomplished something my mother had not. I worked towards my graduation with a desperation that meant I finished months before the school year ended. When I clicked the mouse to shut out the program, all my tests finished and papers completed, I finally felt like I could let go.

That was the day my luck changed. Somehow, a miracle happened. I was given a second chance. One I promised myself I wouldn't waste.

Chapter Two

FAITH

Since I was already at the hospital, I didn't have much to do to prepare for the surgery. They transferred me from the pediatric unit where I'd been staying to the transplant one a couple of floors down so they could get me prepped. The nurses told me it was going to be a few hours before the kidney would be available for transplant. They also warned me that if the kidney didn't meet their standards once it was harvested, then the transplant would be called off. Up until that point, I hadn't thought about the possibility that it would be my turn and I still wouldn't get my kidney.

I spent the next few hours reading, trying with all my might not to focus on the chance that this was a false alarm. That fate would be so cruel as to finally hand me a second chance only to take it away again. The nurses checked back in with me often and when one of them walked in with a huge smile on her face, I knew the news was going to be good. The kidney was healthy and a perfect match so it wouldn't be long before I'd have the transplant.

It had been years since I'd allowed myself to cry. Not since the day I had found my mother dead in our apartment and the rug had been pulled out from under me. I cried tears of joy for the first time in my life. There was no controlling them as they flowed from my eyes and down my cheeks as I sat alone in a hospital bed and learned my prayers had been answered.

But as happy as I was for myself, my thoughts turned to my donor and I hoped when they had passed away that they were surrounded by a family who loved them. Although nobody could hear me, I whispered my gratitude to them softly and promised to honor their sacrifice as best I could. By the time they came and took me to the operating room, I was ready to face my future—whatever might come next.

My confidence held up as we rolled down the corridor. It didn't waver as they hooked me up to all the monitors. Or when the surgeon walked me through what he was going to do during the transplant. None of it was new information because my medical team had already walked me through all of it, insisting I be ready for the surgery when it happened...even though in my mind it had always been *if* and never *when*. But as the anesthesiologist got ready to put me under, my calmness fled in a rush of panic. I'd reached the point where I accepted my own mortality, but I wanted to live.

Desperately so.

Even though I was utterly alone in the world.

But I didn't fully trust the miracle that had been granted to me. There was still a voice inside my head, screaming that things never went the right way. Not for me. That something was about to go horribly wrong with the surgery, and I'd never wake up again.

My distress didn't go unnoticed by the doctors. The surgeon bent low, his gaze locked with mine. "Everything's going to be okay, Faith. I've got you." The confidence in his green eyes was the last thing I saw before the anesthesiologist pushed the drugs into my system and knocked me out.

When I woke up afterwards, I was told the transplant was successful, but that there was one complication. A month prior, I had developed an irregular heartbeat that the doctors had been treating with medication, an atrial fibrillation they'd called it. Apparently, my heart went haywire while I was under, and my blood pressure dropped dramatically. The only way to fix it was to do a procedure they had explained when my heart first started to act up. A procedure that had totally freaked me out.

While I was under, they used metal patches on my chest to pass an electric current to my heart. The current reset my heart's rhythm back to its regular pattern. In other words, they shocked my heart and stopped it to try and make it beat normally again. Luckily, I was knocked out when it happened and the procedure worked without me even knowing about it. They told me my heartbeat went back to regular again after a few minutes. I hoped like hell it stayed that way, and I never had to go through it again since just the thought of the procedure made my heart go haywire on its own.

Before I knew it, I had spent a week recovering at the hospital and they were ready to discharge me. It was hard to believe they had cut me open, put a part of someone else inside me, and were ready to kick me out so soon. To me, it seemed impossible to fathom, but to the medical team, it was just what they did every day.

I only had a few months to go before my eighteenth birthday, and I was petrified about being discharged. I had started to pester Sarah about where I was going to go a few days ago and she just kept telling me she was working on it. They couldn't just discharge me to some random foster home since I still had a lot of recovering to do, so the hospital's discharge planner talked to me about long-term care facilities. They'd be able to provide the around the clock help I needed for a little bit longer. Knowing what most foster homes were like, one of the facilities sounded pretty damn good to me.

The day before I was due to be discharged to the facility, Sarah came for another visit. Our relationship had changed since I had gotten sick. We were on a first name basis, something I'd never seen another caseworker allow with any of the kids under their watch. I knew it was partially because of the guilt she felt for what had happened to me. She had placed me in the home where I had gotten sick and was devastated by the idea that it was her fault for not keeping a closer eye on my foster mother. I had gone through a stage where I had blamed her too, but eventually, I realized it was the system that had failed me and not Sarah.

"Hey, kiddo," she greeted me. "You ready to finally get out of here?"

"That depends on where I'm going."

"Well," she sighed. "I've looked into the facilities your discharge planner recommended, and I've got good news. One of them accepts Medicaid, and they're willing to take you."

"Then get me outta here!"

"Will do," she laughed. "But before you go, I wanted to talk to you about something else."

My body froze, and the smile slipped from my face. I braced myself, waiting for bad news. "About what?"

"Your future."

It wasn't going to be long before I aged out of the system and had to figure out what to do with the rest of my life now that I actually had one to live. But I hadn't given much thought to my future beyond recovering from the transplant—probably because it was damn scary to think about being on my own with only a high school diploma and a strict prescription regimen that I needed to follow. But if Sarah had a plan of some kind, I trusted her enough—just barely, although I'd come to believe in her more than I had any other person before—to at least listen. I offered her a weak smile. "What about it?"

"Have you given any thought to college?" My stunned disbelief must have shown on my face because she hurried to explain, "I know you have a lot on your plate right now, but time is running out if you want to apply. I'd love to wait until you're fully recovered and back on your feet, but you only have two weeks to get everything turned in if you want to start in the Fall with the rest of the freshman class."

"Sarah," I paused, trying to think of a nice way to word what needed to be said. "College just isn't —I couldn't—no, I haven't given any thought to college because I didn't think I was going to be alive long enough to worry about how I'd be able to afford it if I ever managed to get accepted anywhere."

She sat down on the chair next to the bed and leaned forward with her forearms on her thighs. "Then now's the time to start worrying because you are going to live long enough to think about it. And you'll get accepted—you have a solid GPA, high test scores from when you took the SAT last year, and a compelling story to tell in your admission essays."

"But the cost—"

"You didn't listen to a word I said about the state's tuition waiver when I mentioned it to you earlier in the school year, did you?"

"I'm sure I listened"—she snorted, and I couldn't blame her because I didn't sound convincing at all—"since it kinda sorta rings a bell." A super distant one, but a bell nonetheless.

Her hazel eyes gleamed with determination. "Listening and hearing are two completely different things, and I really need you to hear me now."

"Okay." I shifted on the bed, twisting so it was easier to hold her gaze. "You have my full attention."

"You qualify for a full waiver of tuition and fees if you attend a state school." My jaw dropped, and the good news kept coming. "And I'm almost positive I can get you additional financial support through the Postsecondary Education Services and Support program."

"What kind of support?"

Her lips tipped up in a grin. "The kind that will cover the majority of your living expenses while you're in college."

"How much is a majority?"

Her grin turned into a huge smile. "Twelve hundred and fifty-six dollars a month."

"Holy shit!" I fell back on the mattress and stared up at the ceiling, tears filling my eyes and making the view hazy. Free tuition. Enough money to cover my living expenses each month if I was careful. It was more than I could have hoped for, but the pessimistic side of me just had to ask, "What's the catch?"

"Don't age out of the system. Stay in extended

foster care until you turn twenty-one. Get continued case management services and judicial review every six months."

I turned my head and blinked at her. "That's it?"

"That's it."

"Would I be able to keep you as my caseworker?" She nodded, and I swiped at my cheeks as my heart started to fill with hope. "Then that's a downside I could live with." In my situation, it sounded more like a godsend because I was nowhere ready to stand on my own two feet...even if it meant I'd have to go to another foster home.

She reached out and squeezed my hand. "Since it'd only be short-term until you moved into the dorms, I might even be able to get you back into the last foster home you were in before you needed to be admitted to the hospital."

It was like she'd read my mind and already found a solution that more than worked for me. "That would be amazing."

"I can't make any promises, but I'll do my best," she swore. "And if it doesn't work out, I swear to you that I'll find you a good placement. Somewhere you'll be safe."

"Hey," I whispered, reaching out to squeeze her

hand like she'd just done with mine. "What happened to me wasn't your fault."

"Sometimes it feels like it is," she admitted softly.

"You came when I called, no questions asked."

"But—"

"And you made sure the rest of the kids were moved to better homes. Right away," I reminded her.

"I just—"

"Nope." I shook my head and leaned back against my pillows. "No more looking back and thinking 'what if?' because it won't do either of us any good. What happened is already done, and I've been given a second chance. Let's focus on making the most of it."

She heaved a deep sigh before nodding. "The best way to do that is to get you enrolled in college."

"Is two weeks enough time? What all do I need to do to apply?" I'd sat through the usual presentations and talks in high school about college, but I'd never paid much attention because I didn't think it was even a remote possibility for me.

She grabbed the laptop the hospital had been letting me use off the rolling, over-the-bed table and handed it to me. "Figure out which state schools you'd like to attend, go to their websites, and fill out the online applications. I've talked to your guidance counselor who assured me she'd have your transcript ready to send out as soon as you let her know where you're applying."

She bent down, pulled an envelope out of her bag, and held it out to me. "And I wrote a letter of recommendation in case you need one."

Reading it in front of her would have been way too awkward, but I was dying to know what she'd written about me. "What does it say?"

"I told them about your childhood and how you rose above circumstances which would crush some adults. How you've become an amazing young woman despite odds that were stacked against you. And that they would be lucky to have you as a student there because I have no doubt you will find a way to accomplish anything you set your mind to doing."

"You left out the part where I can leap tall buildings in a single bound?" I joked, feeling a little uncomfortable with being the recipient of so many compliments.

She reached out and pretended she was going to take the letter back from me. "I can always add it in if you think it'd improve your odds."

I clutched the envelope to my chest. "Nah! Maybe we'd better leave that part out."

"Since you accepted that so well, I might as well give you this now too," she mumbled, leaning down again to pull another envelope out of her bag and holding it out to me. "This should cover the application fees."

Taking it from her, I peered inside and found a prepaid debit card. "You shouldn't have done that. Can't you get in trouble or something since you're my caseworker?"

"It's not from me." She jerked her chin towards the closed door. "You have a lot of people around here who are rooting for you."

Accepting money from Sarah would have been bad enough, but taking it from the people who'd saved my life? No way. "I couldn't—"

"You can, and you will," she insisted. "I might have been able to get the application fees waived, but with the super tight timeline I'm not sure we have enough time to make it happen. All it took was one brief mention of that concern to your doctor when I asked him if you'd be healthy enough to enroll for the Fall term a few days ago, and one of the nurses handed me that debit card when I got here today. With a huge smile on her face, too."

"Crap," I mumbled. "I'm going to have to accept it, aren't I?"

"That depends on two things." She sat back,

crossed her arms over her chest, and stretched her legs out. "Would it bother you to disappoint everyone who threw in to give you that card? And how badly do you want to go to college?"

The answer to the second question was easy. "Now that I've got a new kidney, a college degree is at the top of the list of things I want." The first question was a little trickier. I'd grown accustomed to not letting other people's feelings matter much to me because mine didn't seem to factor into anyone's decisions but my own. But the nurses and doctors had taken good care of me while I'd been in the hospital. They'd done everything they could to save my life. And they'd been kind to me—even before they'd pulled the money together for me to be able to apply to college. Throwing their generosity back into their faces felt wrong, and I'd made myself a promise a week ago to not let my second chance go to waste. Part of that was doing the right thing whenever possible. "And no, I don't want to disappoint them."

She beamed a smile my way. "Well, then I guess you have some work to do before they come to transport you to the rehab facility."

"I guess I do."

She got up and walked to the door, turning towards me before she opened it. "If you run into any problems, give me a call. I've helped my fair share of kids fill those things out, so I'm a bit of an expert."

"Will do."

It wasn't long before I discovered that filling out college applications was a major pain in the ass. I took Sarah up on her offer and called a few times over the next two weeks. She helped, just like she'd said she would. And she also got me back into the same foster home when I was discharged from the rehab facility. Things were good there, and then they got even better.

My conversation with Sarah that day changed my life—to the point that I almost couldn't believe it was the one I was living. All that studying I had done when I thought I was going to die really paid off when I got accepted into two different state schools. One was in my hometown; the other about three hundred miles away. Since Sarah and the transplant center were in town, I opted to go to the school closer to home.

Sarah was able to line up the tuition waiver and stipend for me, and the days flew by as I marked item after item off my list of things to do. Before I knew it, I was walking across campus for my first day of classes and the excitement was almost overwhelming. I never thought in a million years that I would be able to go to college. Not back when my mom was alive, or when I was living in foster care, and certainly not when I was in the hospital. Yet there I was, a college freshman. Not only had I been given a second chance at life, I'd been handed an amazing opportunity. One that I would do my best to honor.

Luckily, I was used to living with a bunch of strangers, so I was expecting the transition to dorm life to be easier for me than most of the other students. I even sort of had a small support system since there were nine other kids from the foster system enrolled as incoming freshmen. Sarah had even talked the school into pairing me up with one of the other girls as my roommate. As I watched groups of girls giggle and hug while I trudged to the dorm with the textbooks I'd just grabbed at the campus bookstore, I was doubly glad to be matched with someone closer to my own background because I knew I wouldn't ever be able to be as carefree as they were. I just needed to remember that I was happier now than I ever had been before in my life.

My gaze drifted away from the nearest group of girls while I was giving myself a pep talk and landed on a bunch of boys playing football in the quad, the grassy area surrounded by dorms on all sides. I wished I didn't have to walk across it to get to the academic side of campus, but it was what it was I guessed. The guys had divided into two teams, half of them kept their shirts on and the others had gone without. I faltered a bit in my step as my eyes landed on a guy I really wished had been picked to go shirtless.

He ran across the grass to join his team in a huddle. My gaze trailed up his body to take in the dark brown hair which needed a trim, laughing brown eyes, and dimple showing in his cheek. If I had to guess, I'd say he hadn't shaved in a couple days, and the look really worked for him. When he leaned into the huddle, my eyes landed on his ass and I almost groaned out loud. He really was the epitome of tall, dark, and handsome.

Even though I wasn't in the market for a boyfriend, I was tempted to stop and watch them play. Then I heard the group of girls I'd noticed earlier as they whispered about the boys, and I realized it wouldn't matter anyway. My long, dark hair was pulled up in a ponytail, and I didn't even have any mascara on the lashes of my brown eyes. Glancing down at my tattered jeans, flip-flops, and T-shirt, I knew I didn't compare favorably to the rest of the girls who were dressed in short skirts or shorts and tight shirts that showed off a lot of tanned skin and toned muscle. There wasn't a chance in hell I'd be caught dead in anything that showed my legs right now because I still needed to gain back a lot of the weight I'd lost, and I needed to stay out of the sun so there was no tanning for me.

I regretfully tore my gaze away from the football hottie and continued on my way to my dorm, redirecting my focus to what was truly important for me right now—school. I didn't want to worry about the things I didn't have. Instead, I wanted to focus on what I could do with this chance. There was a family out there who suffered a terrible loss from which I benefited. I refused to let them down—not for anything or anyone.

Chapter Three

FAITH

Three Years Later

"YOU'VE GOTTA HAVE FAITH." I'D BEEN distracted while the nurse had asked me the usual questions to kick off my annual check-up appointment, but her whispered words of encouragement made me smile. I'd never asked how the office staff had learned about the tradition started by the nurses when I'd been in the hospital, but it wasn't because I hadn't appreciated the reminder of one of the happier memories from my stay there.

The nurses had gotten into the habit of reminding me that I needed to have faith that things were going to get better each time they checked my vitals. It was how every morning had started for me for months—with a super early wake-up call by one of the nurses to make sure I hadn't gotten sicker during the night while they teased me about my name. I never took offense though because I knew they didn't mean anything bad by it. Although the members of my medical team were aware I was part of the foster system, I didn't think they knew much about my background beyond that. And they definitely didn't know my confusion about my name.

I never understood why my mom picked Faith. She'd given up on hope before I was even born, and having a baby girl sure hadn't changed her outlook. Her approach to mothering didn't inspire flights of fancy—quite the opposite in fact. Growing up with her indifference taught me reality was harsh and dreams were for suckers. That was her gift to me before she died, and the years that followed didn't help much either. Being a cynical girl named Faith was just one of life's little ironies I guessed.

TAKING A DEEP BREATH, I TRIED TO SETTLE MY nerves and flashed the nurse an almost-genuine smile. She gave my hand a gentle pat, and my fake smile turned into a genuine grin. "I wouldn't be here if it weren't for how good you guys are at your jobs. So I do have faith—in all of you."

"Have it in yourself, too. Because we do, and for good reason." She dug a piece of paper out of her scrub pocket and smoothed it open. "Maybe I should ask you to sign this for me so I can say I knew you before you became famous."

My cheeks warmed, and I knew I was blushing. "I'm never going to be famous, not with a degree in social work. But I'll be helping people, which is more important anyway."

"From what I read in the paper"—she folded the article that'd run in Sunday's edition and put it back in her pocket—"you already have."

I wasn't used to compliments, and I looked down at my hands in my lap as I fidgeted on the exam table. She gave my hand another squeeze before she walked out of the exam room and left me alone to wait for my doctor. It was only a few minutes later when he rapped his knuckles against the door and poked his head inside the room. "Everybody decent in here?"

"It's only me; which you know," I chuckled, shaking my head as he came in and shut the door behind him. "Just like you know that I'm decent because it's been a couple of years since I've had to wear one of those awful robes."

"Yeah, but asking never gets old."

Dr. Stewart enjoyed his corny jokes, and I'd quickly gotten used to them when I first started seeing him. "Neither does answering."

"I'm glad you think so." He shook his head as he sat on the stool next to the counter and rolled towards me. "The patient I saw before you did not appreciate my sense of humor."

"A tough audience, huh?"

"Very tough," he sighed. "But I guess I have to cut them some slack since this was only their second post-op appointment with me."

I thought back to how I'd felt after I'd been discharged from the hospital and started to see Dr. Stewart in the outpatient clinic. Even though I'd been staying in a rehabilitation facility and they'd done all the heavy lifting to get me there, the effort required on my part had been enough to exhaust me. "Yeah, some grouchiness is to be expected."

"Indeed." He grabbed his stethoscope and did the usual exam stuff—listened to my breathing, checked my ears and throat, looked for any signs of excessive swelling in my belly and ankles. "You're looking good."

I sat up and scooched to the edge of the table,

my legs swinging because I was trying to burn off nervous energy. Even though my blood tests had been relatively stable with only one minor issue over the past year, I couldn't get rid of the feeling that the other shoe was about to drop. Getting the kidney transplant was one of the few things that had gone right in my life, and it was like I was always waiting for it to go wrong somehow. "How about my numbers? Are they still doing okay?"

He dropped his stethoscope in his lab coat pocket and sat back down, rolling towards the counter on the opposite wall to grab his tablet. After a few taps on the screen, he smiled at me. "They're really good. Your WBC, HCT, and PLTS have remained stable over the past year. Same with your creatinine and BUN. Your electrolytes are right where they should be, so you'll need to keep taking the magnesium supplement. Your Prograf levels have remained where I'd like to see them after the dosage change we made in February, so we don't need to make any additional changes there."

When I'd first gotten sick, I'd barely been able to follow the explanations the doctors and nurses had given me. It was as if they were speaking in a foreign language I'd been desperate to understand because it held the key to my survival. But now I didn't even blink at all the acronyms Dr. Stewart used since I'd gotten used to hearing them and could easily follow along. "Please tell me that means I can go back to doing blood work every three months again."

"I think that can be arranged."

"Yes!" The tension drained from my body, and I pumped my fist in victory. It'd taken me awhile to work my way up to quarterly needle sticks at the lab and annual visits with Dr. Stewart, so it'd sucked when my numbers slipped and he'd made me start going to the lab more often over the past half year.

"Are you sure? I could make you go in every month if you'd prefer," he teased.

I held my hands up in surrender. "No need to threaten me with extra needle sticks. Quarterly is perfect!"

"That's what I thought." The humor leached from his expression, and I braced myself for what he was about to say when he wagged his finger at me. "I know it's your senior year and you'll be busy, but you need to remain as vigilant as ever when it comes to your health. Eat right, take your medications, get plenty of rest, and try to keep the stress to a minimum."

I wrapped my arms around my middle, hugging myself in a protective gesture that was instinctive. I knew Dr. Stewart was only lecturing me because he meant well. He wanted me to stay healthy, but I felt like he was criticizing me, and it made me a little bit defensive. "I promise that I'm doing my best. The food services staff on campus has gotten used to me asking questions about everything they serve. It's to the point where they spout off the sodium content as soon as they see me. When there isn't a great meal option for me, I hit up the salad bar." I jerked my thumb towards the backpack I'd left on the chair against the wall. "I always have a water bottle on me to make sure I'm drinking enough. I've never been to a kegger and barely touch alcohol. But getting enough sleep and avoiding stress is easier said than done when most of my classmates resort to all-nighters to keep up their grade point average."

"I know you're doing your best, Faith," he murmured, offering me an encouraging smile as he leaned forward. "But it doesn't stop me from worrying about you because I also know it's harder for you than most of my other patients because you're on your own without a support system in place."

I couldn't argue his point because it was true. The reason I hadn't been a good candidate for a transplant was because of my home situation, and I was even more alone now than I'd been back then

—but better off for it. I shrugged, hoping he'd take the hint and quickly move past my home life—or lack thereof—as a topic of discussion. Even after all this time, I still hadn't grown accustomed to the doctors and nurses knowing so much about me. With my childhood being what it was, I valued my privacy and didn't open up to people easily.

"Despite the challenges you face, you've thrived since your transplant. Not just medically, but academically too." He lowered his voice like he was sharing a secret with me as he continued, "Don't brag about it out in the waiting room to anyone else, but we consider you our star patient around here."

My cheeks filled with heat again, and this time when I shrugged it was out of self-consciousness instead of uneasiness. "Because of that stupid article? I really wish the school hadn't talked me into doing the interview for it."

"No, it's because you've thrived despite the odds stacked against you. Looking at it from a purely statistical point of view, you weren't a good candidate, but by a twist of fate you got your second chance and proved everyone wrong. My team and I are proud to have been a part of that miracle."

Remembering the desperation I'd felt back then, I swallowed down the lump in my throat. My life had hung in the balance, and there hadn't been anything I could do to control it. My fate had been in the hands of my doctors, and I still wasn't sure how they'd managed to get me a kidney when my score hadn't put me anywhere near the top of the list. "And I'm lucky to have all of you on my side."

"Do me a favor and keep that in mind when one of us wants to talk about that article you're so determined to pretend doesn't exist." I nodded, but he didn't seem convinced. "We feel like we have a vested interest in you."

"Yeah, yeah, yeah," I sighed, making light of their concern because I didn't know how else to respond to it.

"And it isn't every day one of my patients is recognized for their contribution to our community."

I offered him a shy smile. "I think you're overstating things a bit. I'm not out there saving lives like you guys. I'm just helping to educate a small group of high school kids about their college opportunities like my caseworker did for me."

"I think you're minimizing the impact you've had on others. How many of the foster kids starting their freshman year at your college went to a high school you visited?"

My cheeks heated again. "Most of them."

"Maybe you didn't save those kids, but that's almost a hundred lives you've changed for the better."

It was hard to wrap my brain around that number—one hundred and two foster kids had enrolled as freshmen at my school this year. It was a huge increase over the ten of us who'd started there together three years ago, and I couldn't help but be proud that I'd had something to do with it. "I'm just keeping the promise I made the day I was given a second chance—to put the gift I've been given to good use."

Dr. Stewart's kind green eyes narrowed as he searched my face. "Your kidney was a gift, but there's no debt to pay because of it other than to live your life to the fullest. If helping other foster kids is something you want to do, then keep on doing it. But for *you*; not for your donor. Honor their gift by being happy."

"I do like helping them," I assured him. It wasn't just about honoring my donor's sacrifice. Giving back made me feel like I mattered, at least in some small way. But being happy was an utterly foreign concept to me. It just wasn't something I thought about.

I was alive.

I had a roof over my head and food in my belly.

I was close to earning my college degree in social work, my major inspired by the difference Sarah had made in my life and the work I'd done with other foster kids.

Having all of that was a bounty to me. Unexpected and greatly appreciated. But maybe it was time for me to strive for more. To find joy in my life. Somehow.

Chapter Four

FAITH

One week later, I wasn't any closer to figuring out how to find my happiness. I'd been too busy getting myself ready for the start of the new school year and trying to help the group of incoming freshman I'd been working with prepare for their move onto campus. Most days, it felt like a losing battle. They needed so much and had so little. But that didn't stop them from giving me a hard time about being a local celebrity after they heard about that dumb article in the paper. Extra time hadn't helped me with my discomfort over it. And it only got worse when I was called into the public relations office.

"You want me to do what?" I shook my head, giving her the physical equivalent of the verbal response since I knew better than to actually say no to a higher-up at the school. The state might have been the one picking up the tab for my tuition and fees as part of their exemption program for former foster kids, plus the stipend to help with living expenses, but I didn't want to end up on anyone's radar and run the risk of losing it all by getting kicked out of school.

"One of our donors reached out to us after reading your interview in the newspaper. She'd like to have lunch with you today," the PR Director explained again.

Hearing it the second time around didn't help me make any sense out of what she'd told me. "But why?"

"Because she wants to help your incoming students outfit their dorm rooms."

Shit, I was going to have to say yes. Moving onto campus was an exciting time for most students, but it was also stressful as fuck for foster kids because they didn't have the same kind of resources. No family to help with the move-in process. Nobody to take them shopping to buy the myriad of things needed for life in the dorm. Or to take them to the campus bookstore to buy school apparel that proudly proclaimed you were a student here—or even just notebooks, pens, and highlighters. If me going to lunch with some lady meant their transition to college was easier than mine had been, then turning down the offer wasn't an option.

"Count me in. Where and when?"

I barely stifled a groan when she named a fancy restaurant several miles off campus. Meeting a big donor there meant I not only needed to change out of the cutoff shorts and T-shirt I was currently wearing, but I probably needed to put on a dress instead of whatever dressy-ish option I would have thrown together if I'd been meeting her anywhere else. And as if that wasn't bad enough, it wasn't within easy walking distance so I'd have to figure out how I was getting there. Taking an Uber would only cost about fifteen bucks round trip, but it'd still be a hit to my budget in a month when my move-in expenses already made it tighter than it usually was—which was pretty damn tight.

Two hours later, I reminded myself how important the meeting was as I stepped out of the car that'd actually ended up costing me ten bucks one-way. "Looks like I'll be dipping into my savings account sooner than I thought," I grumbled, walking towards the front doors of the restaurant. The building was light years apart from the dive I'd waitressed in over the summer to earn the thousand bucks I'd barely managed to sock away for textbooks and emergencies. I needed it to last until I found a job after graduation, and I'd promised myself I wouldn't touch the money in there unless it was absolutely necessary. I hadn't expected to dip into it quite so soon, but I didn't have a cheaper transportation option that would've worked today.

"It is what it is," I reminded myself. Worrying about it after the fact wasn't going to do me any good, so I pasted a smile on my face as I walked through the doors. "I'm meeting Elaine Montgomery."

The pretty blonde working at the hostess stand looked me up and down before offering me an obviously fake smile. "Right this way. Mrs. Montgomery is already at her table."

Following behind her, I had to work hard to keep my smile on my face. If I wasn't up to snuff for the hostess, what were the odds that a big donor wasn't going to look down on me? I smoothed down the skirt of my dress and took a few deep breaths to try to calm my nerves. When the hostess stopped at a table, the woman seated there thanked her and rose from her seat. The smile she aimed my way was so big, there was no doubt it was genuine. I bit my lip to stifle a giggle at the hostess's baffled expression as she walked away.

"I'm so happy you could make it to lunch,

Faith." She gave me a quick hug before sitting down and waving at the seat across from her. "I hope that wasn't too familiar, but I feel like I already know you after reading that article and speaking to the school about you. And I'm a hugger. It drives my son crazy because I'm always embarrassing him by hugging him and all his friends."

"It's fine, Mrs. Montgomery," I reassured her as I sat down, even though it was unusual for me since I didn't know a lot of people who could be considered huggers.

"Call me Elaine, please."

A hug and a request to use her first name. *Huh.* So far, the big donor who wanted to meet at a super fancy restaurant was way different from what I'd been expecting. I'd thought she'd be uppity and condescending, but I wasn't getting that feel from her at all.

"Will do."

"I always feel so old when someone calls me Mrs. Montgomery." She leaned forward and lowered her voice as she continued, "And it makes me want to look around for my mother-in-law."

"Is she here?" I whispered back.

"Good heavens, no!" she laughed. "She moved to Arizona for the dry heat a couple of years ago, but I still find myself doing it anyway out of habit."

"Mrs. Montgomery, it's a pleasure to have you back again today."

Elaine flashed me a smile, her brown eyes twinkling before her gaze darted up to the waiter. I barely stifled a laugh, feeling like I was in on a secret from the waiter.

"It's lovely to be back again, Steven."

"What can I bring for you ladies to drink?"

"A bottle of sparkling water for the table, a sweet tea for me, and—"

When her attention shifted to me, I asked for water with lemon.

"Can I bring you an appetizer today?"

Elaine looked at me. "Their stacked Caprese salad is fantastic. It has organic tomatoes and buffalo mozzarella, drizzled with balsamic vinegar with fresh basil."

"Sounds great to me."

"The Caprese salad, please Steven. And a few minutes to peruse the menu for our lunch selections."

"Yes, ma'am."

She waited until he walked away to complain, "A 'Mrs. Montgomery' and a 'Ma'am' all in the span of a few minutes. Is it any wonder I feel old?"

Since I'd pictured someone much older when the publicity director had told me I was meeting with a big donor, it was easy to say, "You definitely don't look it."

"Thank you, that's sweet of you to say."

We chatted about nothing important for a couple of minutes before the waiter returned with our drinks and the appetizer.

"Are you sure you don't want something else to drink? An iced tea? A Coke?" she asked after he took our lunch order.

"No, thank you. I don't really do caffeine very often."

"A college student who isn't addicted to coffee? You're even more unique than I thought."

The reason I mostly avoided it was definitely unique for college students. It was important for me to stay hydrated, and caffeine was a diuretic. But I wasn't one to volunteer personal information to people I didn't really know—or even those I did. "That's me. I like to be an original."

"Well, you've certainly accomplished your goal then"—she spooned some tomatoes and mozzarella onto her plate and then nudged the appetizer my way—"since I don't know any other college student who has accomplished as much with their volunteer work as you've done. Most of my son's friends only know what volunteer work is because it was a requirement in high school."

"I didn't really think of it as volunteering since it started out with me just calling my old high school and a couple ones nearby and asking if I could come in and talk to any students they had who were in the foster system," I answered as I served myself. "Something my caseworker had said to me, about not hearing her when she talked to me about the state paying for me to go to college, really stuck with me and I thought maybe I could do something to help other kids in the same situation."

"How did it snowball from there into more than a hundred students enrolled as freshmen this year?"

"That's harder to answer." I paused to take a sip of my water while I gathered my thoughts. "I think most of us didn't hear the information about the programs available to us once we graduated high school because we were focused on surviving each day instead of looking towards the future. Or at least that's what I assumed since that's how it was for me."

"I'm sorry you had to go through that, but you must have come a long way since then to be where you're at today."

I knew I was part of the story, but I didn't want the focus to remain on me or exactly how far I'd come from the day my mom overdosed. "I figured I could talk to them about what going to college meant to me as a foster kid who had aged out of the system. About the opportunities it presented and the doors it opened. The future it would allow me to have—and them too if they were willing to give college a chance."

"I'm assuming they were more receptive to hearing it from you rather than other figures of authority?"

I nodded. "Apparently foster kids are way more open to listening to someone like me than their caseworker because a group of the ones I talked to at the high schools from my old school district signed up to take the SAT and applied for school. When I was a freshman, there were only about ten of us on campus. There were almost twice that many the next year. Word somehow spread between guidance offices, and it wasn't long before I got calls asking me to visit more schools. Things just took on a life of its own from there, and now there's a hundred and two coming in the incoming class this year."

"I have a feeling you're being overly modest."

My cheeks heated as I shrugged and stuffed some tomatoes and mozzarella into my mouth because I didn't know what to say to that. Elaine got the hint, and we polished off the appetizer before the waiter reappeared with our entrees. We talked a little bit about the students I'd worked with who were getting ready to move onto campus the following weekend and what kinds of things foster kids might need that wasn't covered by the tuition waiver and stipend programs. By the time I finished my chicken Caesar salad, Elaine had come up with a plan for what she wanted to do.

"I'd like to do some fundraising for the kids; set up a fund where they'll get gift cards and a little extra cash every month."

I'd been hoping for a little help for the group as they moved into the dorms, and her offer of continued support was more than I expected. "Making the transition from a foster or group home to the college campus can be difficult, so that sounds amazing."

"It wouldn't just be for the freshman class. I'd like to do it for all the foster kids on campus."

"All of them?"

"Yes, it doesn't seem fair for the kids who came before the ones mentioned in the article to be left out just because they're a little older," she explained.

Whoa. It was hard for me to wrap my head around the kind of money it would take to do what she was talking about for a group that big. "I can't tell you how much I'd appreciate it, and so would all the students. You'd be making a huge difference in a lot of lives."

"Oh, I don't know about that." She waved off my compliment as we got up to leave the restaurant. "I'm just raising a little bit of money. You did all the hard work to help get them on campus in the first place."

"It might not seem like much to you, but I can tell you from experience that having some extra cash in your pocket or a gift card to buy a pizza will be a big deal to these kids."

"It won't be much," she warned.

Our standards were on opposite sides of the spectrum so I wasn't certain exactly what she meant by 'not much,' but I did know one thing for sure. "It'll be more than they have right now."

"Then I'll make sure it gets done."

We reached the sidewalk in front of the restaurant, and I pulled out my cell phone to request a ride back to campus.

"They can validate your parking if you need it," Elaine explained, moving towards the Bentley the valet had just parked at the curb. He opened the driver's side door and stepped out, the engine still running and his attention on her.

"I don't have a car." Which was hard to admit when it was obvious she didn't just have a car—she had one that probably cost as much as the state was going to pay in tuition for twenty foster kids to attend college this school year.

"Did a friend drop you off? I'll wait with you until they come back to pick you up."

"No, I took an Uber. But it'll only take a few minutes for another one to show up."

She circled back and opened the passenger door on the Bentley. "Get in. I'll drop you off."

I told myself it would have been rude to decline her offer, but really I just wanted to ride in her car. Between the wood veneer touches, buttery leather on the seat, and deep pile carpets, it felt like being wrapped in luxury. When she pulled into the parking lot on campus, I was reluctant to leave the comfort of the passenger seat. "Thanks for the ride. I appreciate it." And so did my savings account.

"It really was no problem. I needed to stop by the campus bookstore to pick up some stuff for my son sometime this week anyway, so I'll just do that next since I'm already here."

"I didn't realize he was a student here, too. What year is he?"

"A senior, like you."

I'd been laser-focused on my studies and working with foster students during my first three years of school, so I didn't have a big social circle like a lot of the other students. I tried to think of any guys I'd met in class or in the dorms with the same last name as hers, but I didn't come up with anyone. "What's his first name?"

"Dillon."

It still didn't ring any bells. "I don't think I know him."

"I guess that's not too much of a surprise since it's a big campus, but maybe he'll be available to come with me on Friday to drop off the first round of donations to you. I'd love for the two of you to meet."

I was too preoccupied with her casual mention of giving me stuff for the group in such a short amount of time to notice the gleam in her eye when she mentioned introducing me to her son. "Friday is the end of this week. Will that be long enough for you to get everything pulled together for so many students?"

"Absolutely," she replied without batting an eye. "And I plan on making this first round special because I'm well aware of all the stuff kids need when they move into the dorms."

I quickly learned that Elaine Montgomery was a woman of her word when we met up that Friday and she handed me one hundred and seventy-two envelopes to pass out to the kids I was working with when they moved onto campus that weekend. Each one was filled with several hundred dollars in gift cards to Publix, Walmart, Target, and a few different restaurants, plus three hundred in cash. She'd somehow managed to raise more than a hundred thousand dollars in less than a week, but she shrugged it off like it was no big deal and seemed more concerned that her son hadn't been around to come with her so she could introduce us. Go figure.

I enjoyed the hell out of handing them out, that was for damn sure. Running around campus, trying to hunt down all the foster kids was a bit insane, but it was more than worth the effort. Especially when I found two of my favorite incoming freshmen, Emily and Kyle, in the parking lot. "Hey, guys! Everything okay over here?"

Kyle was the first to spot me when he turned around and answered, "Yeah, everything's good."

"It's a big day. I was just having a moment," Emily added as she got out of the car and moved next to Kyle.

"A big day in a totally different way for you two." I grinned and widened my eyes at them while wagging my brows, thrilled that they no longer had to keep their secret. It'd been torture watching the two of them around each other and waiting until they could finally be together. As foster kids living in the same group home for the past little while, they would have risked being separated if anyone had caught on to how they felt about each other. "Since you can finally come out as a couple."

"When exactly did you clue in to our secret?" Kyle asked, narrowing his eyes at me.

"Right about the time you strolled into one of my after-school presentations and asked me if it'd still be possible for you to use the waiver if you started a year late since you hadn't applied in time your senior year."

Emily nodded, but Kyle didn't get what I meant even though it'd made his feelings for her super clear to me at the time. "How'd that give us away? A ton of the other kids there were asking questions about the program."

"You missed all the application deadlines, which told me you hadn't been thinking of going before then and something must have changed your mind. When Emily's eyes lit up like you'd just given her the best gift ever, I put two and two together—"

"And came up with the pair of us," he finished for me.

"Yup," I confirmed. "From then on, it was impossible to miss the way you guys just seemed drawn to each other. You didn't even need to be looking at each other to seem like you were still connected." And it'd made me wish that I could find someone who cared about me as much as these two did with each other.

"Maybe now that you've got so many of us enrolled in colleges across the state, you'll take a little more time for yourself and find the guy who's going to look at you the way Kyle does me," Emily suggested.

"Maybe," I sighed. It was hard for me to picture it actually happening for me, though. "Stranger things have happened—like that stupid article about me in the paper leading to me getting funding for every foster kid enrolled here will get gift cards for stuff like pizza, groceries, and the campus bookstore plus a little extra cash every month!"

When Kyle froze up, I was happy Emily was around to calm him back down and answer for the both of them. "That's awesome. Is there anything we need to do? Paperwork to be filled out?"

I offered her a quick smile. "Nope. I met with the woman in charge of it yesterday, and she gave me a bunch of stuff to hand out to everyone this weekend."

I heaved my backpack off my shoulder and dug through it to pull out two envelopes. Since Kyle didn't reach out to grab his, I handed them both to Emily. I loved how her eyes opened wide when she looked inside. "Can you pass along our thanks, from the both of us?"

"Yeah, we'd appreciate it," Kyle murmured.

"Uh huh, I can tell," I laughed, knowing damn well he could care less if I thanked Elaine for them. "No worries, though. I'll pass along your heartfelt gratitude when I talk to her."

"Please do, because what's in these?" Emily jiggled the envelopes. "Wow. Just wow."

"Yeah, I'm not sure how she pulled it off. It's way more than I expected, even with her telling me the first ones were going to be special because of all the stuff kids need when they move into the dorms. And she did them for all the foster kids enrolled here, not just the incoming freshman. We're talking about a hundred thousand dollars of stuff, and I first talked to her a week ago. I can't even wrap my head around how she was able to raise that much money that quickly."

"It bears repeating, so...wow."

I'd certainly said and thought it myself more than once. "Well, if you two crazy kids are all set, I'm going to try to track down the others. I want everyone to get their envelope as soon as possible so they can grab any necessities they're missing sooner rather than later."

Emily gave me a quick hug but didn't let me leave without saying one last thing. "I know I've said it before, but this bears repeating too. Thank you so much. For everything. I can't believe I'm here, and I owe it all to you."

I felt my cheeks heat and didn't quite know how to respond to her gratitude. "I...umm...You. Gah! You don't owe it all to me. You're here because you deserve to be. Because you worked hard for it. I just gave you the nudge you needed. That's all."

"So not true," Kyle argued as he wrapped his arms around Emily. "You did way more than give us a nudge."

"Him especially," she teased.

"There's no arguing with that," I laughed as I walked away, on the lookout for the rest of the kids so I could make their day in the same way I just had with Emily and Kyle. And I owed it all to Elaine Montgomery.

Chapter Five

DILLON

Three months later

"Hit me," the guy to the left of me requested.

I heaved a deep sigh and barely refrained from rolling my eyes at his stupidity. He was the last seat at the table, in what was called "third base." He was the final player before the dealer, who had a six showing. That queen the player just busted on should've gone to the dealer, except the guy took a card when he should have held at fifteen. He was too much of a novice to know how the game was supposed to be played, and it only took him three hands before he fucked things up for the rest of us.

If I wasn't in the middle of a hot streak when he sat down, I would have gotten up from the table right after we finished the first hand he'd played because it'd been quickly obvious he had no clue what he was doing. The dealer had rearranged his bet for him after he'd put two ten-dollar chips on top of a five when the etiquette was to stack them in with the biggest denominations on the bottom. Less than a minute later, she'd had to rebuke him for touching his chips since you weren't supposed to do that after the bet had been placed and was in the betting box. He'd told her he was going to stay on that hand, instead of sliding his cards under his bet. And he'd done it when he'd been sitting at fifteen while the dealer had a seven showing. It'd been a stupid move, resulting in his loss when the dealer flipped over a king and beat him with seventeen. It'd been irritating, but at least it hadn't impacted my hand.

I was hoping he'd quickly grow tired of the game, but I should've known it wouldn't be long before his bad game play cost me money. After he busted, the dealer drew a five. "Twenty-one."

She swept up all the chips left in the betting boxes. If he'd held, she would have been the one to bust and all of us would've won. Eyeing the stack that was about a quarter of what I'd started with tonight, I gulped down the rest of my beer before standing. I picked up my chips and shuffled through them for the twenty-five dollar one I tossed in front of the dealer for a tip. She gave me an appreciative smile, but it dimmed when I turned my attention to the guy who'd just cost me a hundred bucks.

"Do everyone a favor, yourself included, and switch to one of the five-dollar tables instead."

"Whaddya mean? I got just as much right to play at this table as anybody else," the guy blustered as he got to his feet to face off with me. His gaze swept down my clothes, taking in my designer jeans and a button-down shirt. When he looked up again, his upper lip curled into a sneer. "You got no right to tell me what to do. My money spends just as well as yours."

"You want to lose all your money placing stupid ass bets? Go right ahead. I couldn't care less." The guy edged closer to me, and I held my ground as I jerked my thumb over my shoulder towards the players to my right. "But I do give a fuck when you make mistakes that cost the rest of us money."

"Mistakes?" he scoffed. "Blackjack is a game of chance. Luck decides who wins or loses. Not skill."

"You're wrong. Played well, blackjack is a game

of skill in a casino full of games of chance. If you want to win or lose completely based on luck, then you should pick one of those instead." I waved towards the rows of slot machines lining the wall across from us.

His eyes narrowed and he puffed out his chest. "I didn't come here to play slots. I came for the cards."

"Then you should do like I said and switch to the five-dollar table until you figure out how the game's supposed to be played. Learn when to hit, when to stand, when to double, and when to split," I suggested. "Good players don't just blindly try to get as close to twenty-one as possible. They consider the card the dealer's showing, and they make an educated guess of the eventual outcome so they can play their hand accordingly. If you're going to play at a table where the minimum bet is twenty-five dollars, then at the very least you should know to fucking stand on fifteen when the dealer has a six showing because she's going to take another card."

The guy's face turned ruddy and he was winding up to respond when one of the security guards tapped me on the shoulder. "Mr. Montgomery."

It probably should've bothered me that I'd only been playing at the casino since I turned twenty-one a couple of months ago and I'd been there often enough in that short time for them to know me by name. But it didn't—not when it meant I was a valued customer and the casino's security was quick to step between me and the asshole who I was starting to think was looking for a fight. I should've anticipated being on the casino's radar. Some days I won a whack, others I lost. But I always bet big and only at blackjack because I preferred to play poker at the underground games I'd discovered when I was eighteen. After putting some thought into it, I would've been surprised if I hadn't been on their radar.

"Do you need any assistance?"

The security guy directed his question to me, but it only served to piss the asshole off more than he already was and he was the one who answered. "Yeah, I could use some help getting this privileged dick"—he took a step towards me and stabbed a finger into my chest—"to understand that he can't tell me where I can and cannot play. Last I checked, this was a public place, and I've got the right to do what I want where I want to do it."

"Actually, sir." The guard next to me moved between us as he spoke, while another one came up from behind the guy and grabbed his arm to yank it away from my chest and shoved it behind his back.

"The casino is privately owned and we reserve the right to refuse service to anyone for any reason."

"I'm not the one you should be explaining that to!" the asshole yelled, trying to break free of the security guy's hold. He swung his free arm up and pointed at me. "It's him! He's the one who started shit. Not me!"

"Sir, Mr. Montgomery has been playing here regularly for two months"—knowing I was on their radar was one thing, getting confirmation that they knew exactly how long I'd been playing at the casino was another—"and he's never been involved in an altercation until tonight. With you."

The implication was impossible to miss, and the asshole caught it quickly. "Oh, so just because this is my first time here and he's some high roller, it's gotta be my fault?"

"I'm going to have to ask you to lower your voice and get control of yourself, sir. Or else we'll have to escort you out of the building."

"The hell you will," the guy roared back at the security guard, ripping his arm out of the hold the other one had on him and closing the gap between us to haul off and slam his fist into my cheekbone. He'd moved fast enough to catch me unaware, but the second he connected with me, my instincts took over and I defended myself by throwing a punch of my own. I connected with his jaw and felt the force of the hit radiate through my hand.

It felt good.

Damn good.

Even better than the high of a hot streak at the tables.

But I didn't get to enjoy the euphoric moment for long because the two security guys stepped in a split-second after my fist made contact, and several others surrounded us. The asshole got dragged towards the entrance of the casino by three guys, and I was taken through a set of doors marked "Employees Only" at the back by three more.

I didn't struggle, letting them pull me along without putting up a fight. As soon as we were in the privacy of the narrow hallway with the doors closed behind us, the security guard who'd done all the talking out there released my arm. I lifted my hands up, palms out, to let him know they weren't going to get any trouble from me.

"I was just defending myself, man."

"You should've let us do our jobs, Mr. Montgomery."

"It was pure instinct without any thought behind it." I dropped my hands and shrugged my shoulders. "Hell, I didn't even know I was going to throw that punch until it was already done."

"Next time, step back and let us handle the situation. It's why they keep us around, and we're damn good at our jobs."

My attention locked on his first two words. "Can I take that to mean I'm not banned?"

"Keep your head down, stay outta trouble, leave the fighting to us, and you should be fine." His gaze moved to my cheek, and he shook his head with a low chuckle. "At the very least, we're more likely to be the one giving someone else a black eye than ending up with one of our own at the end of a shift."

I lightly pressed my fingertips against the upper part of my cheek and winced. He was right; a bruise was already forming underneath my eye. "Shit."

"Yeah, that's gonna leave a mark."

The guard smirked at me, but I didn't see the humor in the situation. I wasn't going to be able to hide the bruise from my parents since I was supposed to have dinner with them in less than two hours. They were bound to assume my black eye was connected to gambling since we'd fought about it over the past couple of years. I could try coming up with a convincing cover story, but I was a shit liar when it came to my parents and they were bound to see through it anyway. I was so fucked.

"I'll be sure to leave it to you guys if anything happens again," I promised before walking out the door they'd led me through after the altercation. I kept going, moving quickly through the casino and out to the parking lot since I didn't want to give them a reason to reconsider their decision to let me come back again. Although the rush of punching that asshole had felt damn good, it wasn't worth losing my gambling fix. And that's just what it was for me.

A fix.

A high.

And if you asked my parents, one I needed to avoid like the plague because I was perilously close to becoming addicted. But I wasn't. I had it under control. Completely. I just enjoyed the escape gambling gave me, and it was a hell of a lot better than turning to alcohol or drugs instead.

To anyone on the outside looking in, I had everything a twenty-one-year-old guy could possibly want. Great parents. Good grades. A brand-new car. Money. A killer internship and more job prospects than I knew what to do with. But it was only because they didn't look too deep. Either that or I did too good of a job at hiding the pain I struggled with each and every day.

Chapter Six

FAITH

"I need your help."

I'd met with Elaine Montgomery a total of five times, including the lunch when we'd first met. Over the course of three months, she pulled together almost two hundred and fifty thousand dollars to donate to the foster kids attending my school. Her version of "not much" had turned out to be two hundred dollars per student on an ongoing basis, split between cash and a variety of gift cards.

During that time, she'd texted me a bunch of times to check in. She usually started out by asking if there was anything specific the kids needed. Like last month, she made sure one of the gift cards was to a local Halloween store so everyone could get costumes. There were a lot of themed parties on campus, and she didn't want any of us missing out on the fun just because we couldn't afford to dress up like everyone else. She'd also arranged for us all to get a big discount so our purchases were super affordable. I'd even gotten in on the action, dressing up like a Disney princess. And not even a slutty one to the horror of the girls I hung out with that night. But it was the first time I'd ever had a real Halloween costume, and I figured I'd might as well live out one of my childhood fantasies if I was going to spend money—even if it was someone else's—on something like that.

But our text conversations slowly morphed from all business into something more personal over time. Elaine made sure to ask how I was doing. If I'd done any more visits to local high schools. She'd even gotten in the habit of quizzing me on the boys in my life; or the lack of them really since I wasn't dating anyone.

Although we'd grown closer, she only ever called when she wanted to arrange to meet up for an envelope handoff. And the last time was just a few days ago. Otherwise, she stuck to texts, so having her call unexpectedly let me know something serious was going on even before her request.

She'd never asked for anything in return for her

generosity, until now, and there was only one answer I could give. "Whatever you need."

"My son got into a spot of trouble."

"Okay." With just one word, I managed to convey my confusion about how I could help him. The Montgomerys had money. Lots of it. I'd only managed to keep my savings at its thousand-dollar balance because Elaine insisted on including an envelope for me each time we met. I couldn't conceive of a situation where I'd be able to fix something their money couldn't handle.

"Our family"—she paused, clearing her throat as though it was hard to get the next words out—"suffered a loss a few years ago. We've all struggled with it, but Dillon had a hard time finding a coping mechanism that helped him through the grief. When he started gambling, we tried to be understanding about it. We figured it was better than binge drinking or drugs. Or less risky, at least."

I flashed back to the dingy living room where I'd found my mom's lifeless body. "I've seen what drugs can do to a person, and less risky is an understatement."

"He seemed to have it under control, for the most part. He's barely dipped into his trust fund to pay back his losses. We thought maybe he was winning enough that he didn't get in too deep, or he had it under control enough that he was able to limit the gambling to his monthly allocation from the trust. I'm not entirely certain because it always turned into a huge argument whenever we brought it up with him, and we were worried about pushing too hard. We didn't want to risk him pulling away from us completely. It would destroy his father and me."

I didn't live in a world where things like trust funds and monthly allocations fit into everyday conversation. Or where people cared enough to ask questions, let alone backed off because they were worried about pushing a loved one away. It sounded to me like Elaine's son had no idea how good he had it. He was probably an entitled jerk, but I'd still help if I could because his mom was anything but that. She was kind, generous, and clearly concerned about her son. "You said he got into trouble? What happened?"

"He showed up to dinner on Sunday night with a black eye and said it was because some hothead got in his face at the casino." She heaved a deep sigh before continuing. "He tried telling us that it wasn't a big deal, but it wasn't just a black eye. His knuckles were red and a little swollen too, which means the gambling has gotten bad enough that now he's getting into fights. We were willing to give

Dillon his space before because we thought he hadn't let it go too far. But we can't afford to ignore a warning sign like this and let things get worse. So his father and I have put our proverbial foot down."

"Is that where I come in?" I still had no idea how I could help with any of what she was describing.

"Yes, we told Dillon that he needs to give back to the community by volunteering, and I was hoping you'd let him work with you."

Huh. I hadn't seen that request coming, but maybe I should have. "Like a kind of probation? Where he has to do enough hours to make you worry less about the fight he got into?"

"Yes," she confirmed. "One enforced by us, but it isn't his freedom that's at risk—it's his trust fund."

I didn't know how much money was in that account, but I was willing to bet it was more than I'd ever earn in my lifetime. So there was a lot at stake for her son. He would probably be on his best behavior if I came up with a way for him to help out. Which I was going to do since it was Elaine asking. But still, I wanted to cringe at the idea of being responsible in any way for a guy who had so much but seemed to care so little. "How much time did you want him to spend volunteering?"

"As much as you'll let him," she sighed. "But I

don't want to be too much of a bother. I know you're already juggling a challenging course load, everything you do for the students on campus with you, plus high school visits to encourage more foster kids to apply next year."

"Elaine," I bit out to get her attention since she was on a roll with all the reasons I should say no to what she was asking me to do. "Just tell me what you need, and we'll figure it out."

"Are you sure?"

If I hadn't already been positive after everything she'd done for me and all the foster kids on campus, seeing how worried she was about being a bother would have been enough to convince me. "I'm one hundred percent certain."

"Okay. Great. I think this will work."

It sounded like she was trying to convince herself of that more than me. "I'm sure it will; once we figure out exactly what 'this' is."

"As a parent, you do everything you can to protect your children. To keep them safe."

If only that were true for all parents. My head dropped low, and I squeezed my eyes shut as though it would block out the reality of how different my mom and Dillon's were. My mother had never been concerned for my safety. She sure hadn't done anything to protect me, either. Dillon was damn lucky his mom and dad wanted to keep him safe because so many others certainly didn't care about their kids. I was surrounded by the proof of that sad fact each and every day.

"You give them every advantage you can, and in our case, we had a lot to give Dillon and..." she trailed off. I got the impression she was holding back tears. I wasn't great with handling people who were crying since I tended to wall up my own emotions and didn't share them with others. So I waited, feeling super awkward, until she pulled herself together and continued.

"By spending time with your group, I'm hoping Dillon will get to know some of you. Become familiar with your stories. See that there are people in this world who've faced overwhelming obstacles and come out ahead."

Ouch.

I finally got exactly what she was asking of me. The foster kids were going to be an example to the golden boy. To scare him straight, or something like that. I hated to admit it, but it stung a little knowing why she'd reached out to me for help. I thought she'd come to see me as more than just a foster kid. That we'd gotten to know each other and she saw me as the person I was trying so hard to become.

But I did what I always did and buried the pain,

refusing to show her that she had the power to hurt me. Instead, I focused on injecting some positivity into my tone when I answered. "I can see how it'd work that way. We definitely have our fair share of kids with sob stories who've accomplished a lot that might be able to inspire him."

"Oh! I didn't mean—"

I must not have done as good a job at hiding my hurt as I thought. Either that, or Elaine had gotten to know me better than I expected.

"It's okay," I interrupted her. "According to that stupid article the newspaper insisted on running, I'm apparently pretty good at motivating people. So you might have come up with a brilliant plan."

"Hey, now. The article couldn't have been that stupid since it's how I heard about what you'd accomplished," she reminded me. "And yes, it certainly crossed my mind that I couldn't do much better than having my son spend time with you."

That compliment helped ease the sting from earlier.

A lot.

I laughed softly—and awkwardly—before she hurried to explain further. "Don't get me wrong, Dillon's a good boy. Or man, really, since he's twenty-one. But he's a little lost right now, and I need to do something to try to find a way to stop his downward spiral before he finds himself in real trouble."

I wasn't convinced that hanging out with me and the other foster kids was going to make a difference for her son, but I was definitely willing to try. "Let's see if I can help with that. Maybe he'd like to come with me tomorrow to my old high school? I'm supposed to be there at three, and it'll probably take less than two hours since some of the kids already applied for early decision and are just waiting to hear back if they got accepted. I'll mostly be working with a group of seniors who're prepping to take the SAT early next month since they decided late that they wanted to try for college. It's the last test they can take that'll get scores to the schools by the application deadline."

"That sounds perfect. Maybe he could even help them with some of the math questions since that's his minor."

"That'd be great since math definitely isn't my area of expertise." I'd had other reasons in mind when I'd decided to study social work, but I sure hadn't minded that the number of math classes I had to take was limited. "What's his major?"

"Finance."

"Finance and math? He must really like numbers."

"It's a lucky thing he does since his dad would love to be able to hand The Montgomery Group over to him someday."

Lucky was an understatement since the company Elaine's husband owned was an asset management company with something like forty billion dollars that they managed. I'd gotten curious about her after she'd handed over the first batch of envelopes to me, and any resistance I might have felt at accepting one for myself disappeared when I saw that figure. It wasn't much of a surprise to hear they wanted to keep management of a company that big in the family.

"Will my plans work with his class schedule?"

"Yes, he's done at two-thirty on Tuesdays and Thursdays, and he can drive the two of you over there so you don't have to take a rideshare."

"Are you sure he'll be okay with that?"

"Oh, yes." She didn't hesitate, not even the tiniest bit. "If I tell him to meet you outside your dorm, he'll be there."

"Then I guess I'll finally meet your son tomorrow."

"If only it was under better circumstances."

"It'll be fine," I reassured her. And if it wasn't, at least I'd save the cost of the rideshare to the high school and back to campus.

Chapter Seven

FAITH

After a killer pop quiz during my Integrative Practice Seminar class, the last thing I wanted to do was spend the next two to three hours with a rich guy who had some kind of a chip on his shoulder, even if he was Elaine's son. But a promise was a promise, and I liked to keep mine. So when he finally showed up in his Porsche Cayenne SUV, almost ten minutes later than we'd arranged, I was pissed.

I barely waited for the vehicle to come to a complete stop before I flung the passenger side door open and climbed in. I dropped my backpack on the floor near my feet and fastened my seat belt before turning to look at him. Unlike when I'd gotten a ride from his mom the day I met her, I didn't take the time to enjoy the luxurious surroundings because I barely even noticed them. Instead, I glared at him like I was getting paid to do it. And I had to work hard to keep the scowl on my face. Although it was easy to ignore how awesome his car was, it was impossible to miss all of the hotness that was Dillon Montgomery.

His dark brown hair still looked like it needed a trim. His brown eyes weren't laughing at the moment, but I remembered exactly what they looked like when they did. And I knew right where his dimple popped in his cheek when he smiled. There was no mistaking it—Elaine's son was the football hottie I'd drooled over my first day on campus.

Holy shit.

"You'd better be Faith, or else my mom is going to be even more pissed at me than she already is if I'm not only late but picked up some random chick by mistake."

"I'm Faith."

"And I'm Dillon." He shot me an unhappy look as he pulled away from the curb. "Something you should have confirmed before you climbed into my car. I could've been a total stranger."

I forced myself to ignore the little thrill the flash of heat in his dark eyes gave me and flicked up my index finger to count off all the reasons he was completely wrong. "There are very few Porsche SUVs on campus." My first point was made, and I moved on to the second. "Let alone silver ones that would pull up in the exact place where I was supposed to meet you." His hold on the steering wheel tightened as I added a third finger to my count. "And your mother told me what kind of car you drive."

"Still."

"Still nothing." I dropped my hand into my lap, curling it into a fist. "I might be smaller than you and a girl, but I've been taking care of myself for a long time. I'd be willing to bet that I have a lot more experience at judging people and situations than you do."

"Shit," he groaned. "I really put my foot in it, didn't I?"

"Maybe a little bit." I glanced down at his shoes, which had to at least be a size twelve, and tried not to think about exactly how big those feet were. And how they might correlate to the size of other, more interesting, parts of his anatomy. My cheeks heated, and I quickly jerked my gaze up to his face.

"I'm sorry. My mom told me you were a foster kid, and that's why you work with high school students in the foster system to get them into college."

I hadn't expected him to be the kind of guy who apologized for something small like that, and it melted away most of my irritation from earlier. But it came right back when his attention shifted to the screen on the dash after there was a quick dinging sound.

"Hold on a second, I have a new text message."

"Aren't you in enough trouble already? Texting while driving is dangerous and illegal," I huffed in irritation.

"Only if you're looking at your phone while doing it," he disagreed as he pressed a button on the screen and a voice came through the speaker system to ask if he wanted it to read his messages or compose a new one. Dillon told it to read his messages, and the text message Elaine had just sent was played.

I turned my head and stared at the screen on the dash, surprised to see it looked so much like the one on an iPhone. Once the message was complete, the system asked if Dillon wanted to reply.

"Yes," he answered.

"Go ahead."

Dillon rattled off a response to Elaine's text, the car read it back to him, and he confirmed the message could be sent. Admittedly, I didn't have a lot of experience with luxury cars, but the system in Dillon's SUV seemed excessive. And impressive. I'd never seen anything like it before and didn't even realize it was possible.

"You have Siri in your car?"

"It has an Apple CarPlay system that connects through my iPhone. It was a selling point that helped convince my parents to buy it." He paused, and a muscle in his jaw jumped before he continued, "They're big on car safety features."

"It's pretty cool."

"Yeah."

I wasn't sure why, but the conversation fizzled out from there and we rode in silence the rest of the way to the high school. When we got there, I pointed out where he should park and we headed inside together. We were only a few minutes late, and the group of students I was meeting with were gathered in the classroom waiting for us. I hadn't thought about what they'd read into me bringing Dillon along until I saw the speculation in the eyes of the students I'd gotten to know a bit over the past few months. A few of the girls were looking him up and down like he was a male stripper about to start a performance. And the guys sitting closest to them puffed up like a bunch of pissed off peacocks because they'd lost the attention of the girls to a bigger, hotter, older guy.

"Okay, everybody. I can see that you've already noticed we have a visitor today." Dillon followed me to the front of the room. "This is Dillon Montgomery. He's going to be helping me out from time to time so you might see him around again."

"How'd you guys meet?" one of the girls asked, eyeing him up and down.

"We're both seniors at Southeastern Florida State," Dillon answered. When I glanced at him, he gave me a small shake of his head. I figured he didn't want me to mention his mom was the one getting all the donations for the foster kids who were also students at our school. The kids already knew about it, but I hadn't mentioned the name of the woman behind it all so he was clear on that front. I understood his desire to keep that fact to himself, and I gave him a nod.

"And Dillon is a genius at math, so I thought he could work with those of you who need some help in that area on SAT prep."

A chorus of groans echoed around the room, the usual response to the mention of anything related to math.

"Hey, now," Dillon chided. "Math isn't that bad."

"Good luck convincing them of that," I laughed before getting him setup at a table with the group of students who were scheduled to take the SAT next month. Then I joined the other kids and looked over the progress they'd made on their college applications. It took about an hour to answer all their questions and work through any issues they had. After I sent them on their way, I walked over to where Dillon was still working with the other group.

"Thanks for the help, man. You should be a teacher or something. I learned more in an hour with you than I did all year long in math class," Ian told Dillon as he shoved his stuff into his backpack. He was a basketball player who hadn't gotten a scholarship to a division one or two team and thought that meant he had no chance at a college education. Now that he knew he could get his tuition covered by the state, he was hoping to get accepted to at least a DIII team so he could get some time on the court while he earned his degree. "But I still gotta say it; I don't see how any of it relates back to real life."

"C'mon, dude. You said you play basketball, right?"

"Yeah."

"You might not realize it, but you use a ton of

geometric concepts while playing the game." Dillon leaned forward, his dark eyes gleaming with excitement. "The dimensions of the court, diameter of the hoop and ball, and length from the three-point line to the hoop are all standard measurements for any basketball court. Then there's the path the basketball will take when you take a shot, which is dependent on the angle at which it's shot, the force applied, and the length of the player's arms. Geometric principles are why you need a smaller angle when you shoot from the free throw line than a field goal. And statistics are essential for analyzing a game and determining individual strengths and weaknesses."

"I love basketball, but it ain't exactly real life unless you're drafted into the NBA and making millions," Ian pointed out.

"Are you still gonna play, even if you never get drafted?"

"Hell yeah, I am. My foster mom likes to joke that I was born with a basketball in my hand, and I'll probably be buried with one in it too." Ian chuckled, shaking his head.

"Then it's real life for you."

"Yeah, I guess you're right. But that's just me."

"Okay. But if you look hard enough, you'll probably be able to find math in most things. Take me for example." I took a step closer, curious about what Dillon would choose to share with the kids about his personal life. "I'm a fan of blackjack, which is all about math."

He pulled a deck of cards out of his pocket and laid them face up on the table. "It's based on conditional probabilities. What you've already seen affects what you're going to see. If an ace is dealt, that's one less available." He pulled an ace out of the deck and set it to the side. "Knowing how the cards are going to be dealt works to a player's advantage because asking for a card is one of the only decisions that's entirely up to us. But the dealer doesn't have the same freedom. They have to take one if the total of their cards is below seventeen, and they can't take one if it's between seventeen and twenty-one. So lower value cards favor the dealer because it's less likely they'll bust." He pulled out an assortment of twos, threes, and fours. "The opposite is true for picture cards. They favor the player because the more of them left in the deck, the more chances there are for the dealer to bust."

Ian asked the question I figured we were all thinking. "Dude. Are you talking about counting cards?"

Dillon shrugged his shoulders, shuffling the cards together before putting them back in his pocket. "Unless you have a photographic memory, you can't count all the cards because casinos typically use six to eight decks at a time. But some players develop techniques to help them keep track, and they use math to do that too. They might keep a running tally by assigning a value every time they see a card. Plus one for cards two through six. Minus one for picture cards, aces and tens. No change for seven through nine. A high tally would favor the player because it means more face cards remain than lower value ones, and they'll place their bets accordingly."

"Okay." I walked around the table and placed my hands on Dillon's shoulders, absently noting how muscular they were. "I think that's enough math lessons for today."

Dillon twisted his neck and flashed me an apologetic grin over his shoulder. Unwanted butterflies swirled in my belly, and I quickly yanked my hands away from his shoulders and took a step backwards. His eyes flashed with male satisfaction and his grin grew wider. Determined to ignore the impact he had on me, I shifted my focus to the students. "Your test date is coming fast, so you'll need to squeeze in as much extra study time as you can without neglecting your regular coursework. Maybe set aside some time during Thanksgiving break when you don't have as much homework."

"Ugh. Studying over break sucks," one of the girls complained.

"Yeah, but you guys are in the homestretch. This test score is one of the last things you need to get into college. Trust me, it'll be worth the extra effort."

"I guess if you could get into college while recovering from a transplant, then the least I can do is a little bit of studying over a holiday break that isn't even that big of a deal since I don't have a family to celebrate it with anyway."

The other kids nodded in agreement, and I snuck a peek at Dillon while everyone finished packing up. His brown eyes were wide with shock. I quickly looked away before he could ask me anything, and focused on saying my goodbyes as the kids all headed out. We both kept quiet—for which I was incredibly grateful—as Dillon helped me clean up the room. When we were back on the road, I turned to him and asked, "Were you really teaching my kids how to count cards?"

His lips tilted up at the edges. "Maybe just a little."

"It's a good thing none of them have any money to gamble or else they might learn to enjoy blackjack as much as you do." His lip tilt turned into a full-fledged grin, and I glared at him. "I don't know why you're grinning at me! Look at what your affinity for gambling got you."

"What?" He pointed at his face. "The black eye?"

"Yeah, for starters."

His grin grew into a blinding smile. "It was worth it."

"What? Why?"

"Because it's the reason I met you."

Shit. Those damn butterflies took flight in my stomach again.

Chapter Eight

FAITH

I pressed my hand against my stomach, hoping to get those butterflies to settle down. Dillon's gaze slid to where it rested before he looked out the windshield towards the road again. "You hungry?"

"What?" I shook my head, hoping it'd help clear up the dazed feeling I was experiencing.

"By the time we make it back to campus, it'll be close to dinner time. I figured since we're already out, maybe you'd want to stop and grab some food instead of being stuck with whatever they're serving in the cafeteria tonight."

"I—"

He didn't give me the chance to shoot his suggestion down. "I remember how bad it sucked when I lived on campus, eating so many meals there. My friends and I used to head over to my house a few times a week just to get away from it and catch a home-cooked meal."

"It's not that bad." When he snorted in disagreement, I rushed to defend my opinion. "It really isn't. I mean, the entrees aren't always that great. And they tend to be high in sodium, but the salad bar is actually pretty good."

His gaze slid towards me again. "You need to watch your sodium?"

I hated when I slipped up around people who didn't already know about my illness. "Yeah, I was pretty sick a few years ago, and it's one of the things I need to do to stay healthy now."

"Is that what that girl meant about you getting a transplant?"

I'd been relieved that he'd let the mention of my transplant drop while we'd been in the classroom, hoping he'd take the hint and not bring it up again. But apparently I wasn't that lucky, and he was just waiting for the right time. When we were alone. And I could feel extra awkward talking about it. Having the conversation with only the two of us felt different. It was probably because my transplant was just another part of my life story when I was talking to other foster kids about overcoming our struggles and moving on to get a college education.

"Yeah, but it was a few years ago."

"Still, a transplant is a major surgery, right?"

"Definitely," I mumbled, looking out the passenger side window and thinking about how difficult my recovery had been.

"With a long hospital stay?"

I turned to look at him, surprised by the question. It wasn't what most people thought to ask when they found out I'd had a transplant. "Yeah, I was there for a couple of months before the surgery and then another week afterwards before they discharged me to a rehab facility."

"They sure do like to rush you out of there as soon as they can, don't they?"

I was just as surprised by his answer as I was the last question he'd asked me. "It sounds like you're speaking from experience."

He nodded, clenching his jaw and making that muscle jump in it again. "It wasn't as long as the months you spent in one, but I was stuck there for more than a month after I was in a serious car accident my senior year of high school."

"Oh." I thought about how he'd mentioned his parents being big on car safety, and it suddenly made sense. "I'm sorry. I didn't know. Your mom never mentioned it."

"I'm sure she didn't. It's not something any of us are very comfortable talking about."

"I can understand that." And respect it, too.

"You probably get it more than my friends do."

That was putting it mildly since there wasn't much about my life that I was comfortable talking about with most people. It was ironic considering how much time I spent talking about my past with foster kids in high school. But what I was doing with them meant enough to me that I pushed past the discomfort because I knew I had to share if I wanted to make a difference with them. And I knew they wouldn't judge me because of my past.

Dillon turned into the parking lot for a locally owned Italian restaurant near campus. I'd heard good things about it, but I hadn't eaten there since they were supposed to be on the pricier side. It was rare for me to eat out, and when I did, I was careful picking the restaurant so I didn't spend too much money. "What are we doing here?"

"Grabbing dinner."

"But I didn't say yes when you asked about it."

"You didn't say no either," he pointed out as he pulled into a parking spot and turned off the engine.

"Only because you cut me off and didn't give

me the chance to tell you I was fine with eating dinner on campus."

"C'mon, you know you'd rather have some homemade pasta instead of whatever crap they're serving in the cafeteria tonight," he coaxed.

"But I—"

"Take a whiff. You can smell how delicious it is from here, even with the doors and windows closed."

I breathed in, and the scent of garlic, tomatoes, and olive oil filled my nose. "Oh, wow. It does smell good."

"It tastes even better."

"Fine," I huffed. "I guess I can eat some pasta for dinner tonight."

Dillon waited until we were on the sidewalk, and he was guiding me through the restaurant's front door before he responded. "It's a good thing you agreed because there was no way I was leaving here without eating the fuck out of some Italian food."

Startled laughter burst out of me, and I glanced up to find his brown eyes were filled with humor—just like they'd been when I'd spotted him on campus my first day of school. And damn if it didn't make my heart race like it had back then...but that didn't mean I wasn't going to give him a hard time.

"What would you have done if I'd refused?"

He bent his head low before answering. "If the sniff test hadn't worked, I would have told you I couldn't resist ordering myself some takeout to bring home with me. Not when I was this close to one of my favorite restaurants."

"Did you think I wouldn't be able to deny you one of your favorites?" I whispered back as the hostess approached us with two menus in her hands.

"Table for two?" she asked.

"Yes, please," he replied.

"Right this way."

We followed behind as she led us to a booth in the back corner of the restaurant.

"I was hoping you wouldn't be able to," Dillon said after we were seated.

"Hoping I wouldn't be able to what?"

"Deny me a meal from my favorite restaurant."

"Ah, yeah." The heat of his hand on my lower back as we'd walked across the restaurant had scattered my brain cells. "That."

A busser came over and poured ice water into the glasses in front of us and left a basket of bread with butter on the table.

"I would have made it worth your while, though."

A vivid image of exactly how he could've done that popped into my brain—one involving both of us naked—and I almost choked on the sip of water I'd just taken. "Pardon?" I asked once my coughing fit was over.

"I was going to add a few of their best dishes to my order so you'd have plenty of food to take back to your dorm with you." He widened his dark eyes, pretending to be all innocent, but the wicked gleam in them gave him away. "Why? What'd you think I was going to say?"

"Exactly that," I muttered, opening up my menu to hide behind it while I searched for options that best fit my diet.

"Uh-huh. Sure it was," he chuckled. "I'm willing to place a high stake bet that your idea for how I could do it was a hell of a lot more interesting than mine."

My cheeks heated as I thought about how that would only happen if he could've found someone to bet against him, and it sure as hell wouldn't have been me. Luckily, he let the subject drop and offered me suggestions for the best items to order. My mouth watered at the manicotti and lasagna listed on the menu, but all that cheese and tomato sauce meant their sodium content was pretty high. I might've risked ordering one of them, but the pasta primavera sounded pretty good, too. It was a safer option; pasta with lots of sautéed vegetables and grilled chicken breast in an olive oil based sauce with some fresh, chopped tomato. But I still let out a little whimper when Dillon ordered the lasagna.

"You can have a bite of mine if you'll give me a taste of your pasta," he offered. "I've never ordered that one before."

"Sure, that'd be great."

"Other than watching your diet, is there anything special you need to do because of the transplant?"

I didn't like talking about my medical care with anyone other than my doctor, his nurses, or Sarah. So it was a surprise when I found myself answering his question without any additional prodding on his part. "I'll be on anti-rejection meds for the rest of my life, and I'll always have to wear this"—I pulled the medical alert tag I wore on a necklace out from under my shirt so he could see it—"just in case something happens because the meds make me immune-suppressed."

"That isn't too bad."

"It really isn't," I agreed, finally giving in to the lure of the bread basket and pulling out a warm slice. I slathered it with butter, took a small bite, chewed, and swallowed before I continued. "Everything else is pretty manageable. Regular exercise, eating healthy, limiting my exposure to the sun—things like that."

He nodded and rubbed the left side of his chest. "I guess I was lucky when it came to that at least."

"What do you mean?"

"Other than some mild pain meds for a short amount of time, I didn't have to take anything after I was discharged from the hospital. Exercising and eating healthy"—he flashed me a grin—"or at least mostly healthy, aren't too much of a problem for me because I was pretty serious about football back when I was in high school. So it wasn't much of a lifestyle change for me."

"I get what you're saying, but I count myself very lucky to be taking those pills each and every day. There are more than eighty thousand people waiting on the transplant list, and seventeen of them die every day."

"Shit," he hissed, rearing back in his seat.

"Yeah, I should have been one of those seventeen, but somehow a miracle occurred for me."

"Thank fuck for that."

I liked how that came out. Low. Raspy. Heartfelt. "You can say that again."

"How about I just say that I'm glad you got your miracle."

I liked that even more, but I wanted to lighten the mood a little and thought back to that day I'd first seen him again. "You aren't serious about football anymore?"

"No, my injuries were too extensive. College football wasn't in the cards for me."

He seemed so sad that I found myself apologizing. "I'm sorry. That must've been hard for you."

"It wasn't losing football that was hard, it was—"

The waiter chose that moment to appear with our orders, and the moment was lost. I was too distracted by the ridiculously delicious smells coming from our plates to remember what we'd been talking about by the time the waiter offered us grated parmesan, refilled our waters, and left us alone.

I popped the rest of my bread into my mouth and spooned a portion of my dish onto his empty bread plate. He did the same for me with his lasagna, and I savored it before digging into my pasta primavera. We were fairly quiet as we devoured our food...right up until the waiter dropped off the check and I pulled some cash out of my purse. It sucked to plop that much down on dinner when I could've eaten at the cafeteria for free, but I figured I still came out ahead since I hadn't needed to pay for a rideshare, the food was way better than what I would've gotten at school, and I'd actually enjoyed getting to know Dillon since he was different from the entitled jerk I'd expected.

"You've met my mom, so it shouldn't come as a surprise to you that she'd kill me if I didn't pay when I took a girl out for dinner," he explained as he slid several bills into the black portfolio and handed it to the waiter, pushing my money back to me.

"But this isn't like that."

"Isn't like what?"

I waited until we were outside to answer since it seemed rude to have a discussion while we were walking past other tables of people enjoying their meals.

"I'm sure your mom would understand since it's not the same as if you'd asked a girl to dinner on like a...date."

Dillon chuckled low, shaking his head as he pressed the button on his key fob to unlock the car and opened the passenger side door for me. I didn't understand what he found so funny until he'd gotten in, pulled out of the parking lot, and decided to explain it to me. "It's exactly like that, Faith."

"It's not," I insisted.

"Did I ask you to come to dinner with me?"

"Well yeah, but—"

"Are you a girl?"

"Of course I am."

"Am I a guy?"

"Yes," I huffed.

"Then how is this not a date?"

Well, hell. I'd gone out on a date with Dillon Montgomery and hadn't even realized it was happening until he clued me in right before he dropped me off at my dorm.

Chapter Nine

DILLON

My mom eyed my athletic shorts and shirt, shaking her head. "Maybe you'd like to wear something a little nicer for a change?"

"Nah, I'd just get it all dirty." I jogged over and gave her a kiss on the cheek before dropping down onto the bottom step to pull on my shoes and lace them up. "Dad and I are going outside to throw the football around for a bit before you need our help."

"Help," she snorted. "Is that what we're calling it when you two sneak turkey from the carcass and devour an entire can of black olives before I can even get the food on the table?"

"Hey! We help you bring everything from the kitchen to the dining room table," I reminded her.

"True."

"It's not like you'd let us do any more than that."

"Also true," she agreed.

"And we both know Dad would just set something on fire if you let him help with the turkey."

Our gazes met, identical brown eyes widening, and we both burst into laughter as we thought about how my dad tried to deep fry a turkey last year. We'd been lucky that he'd set everything up in the backyard, or else he would've burned the whole house down. As it was, he'd had to hire a landscaper to come in and redo a huge section of the yard because he'd scorched the grass so badly that no amount of water and sunshine would have fixed it. It'd been one hell of a mess, and we'd ended up eating Chinese takeout for dinner because we didn't have a backup turkey and the side dishes my mom had made wouldn't have been enough for a whole meal.

"I'm so glad we can laugh about it now." My mom wiped the tears from her cheeks. "Because we certainly didn't back then."

"Yeah, you were beyond pissed that he didn't just let you make it the way you always did." I rubbed my abs. "And my mom and I weren't happy to miss out on our all-time favorite meal."

"I think I was angrier with myself for not just

buying a second turkey the minute he suggested deep frying it. I should have known better."

"Yeah, you should have," I teased.

"It's not like you're any better in the kitchen than your father."

"Nope, but I blame my mom for that."

She took the dish towel she'd been holding and snapped me with it in the leg.

"Hey!" I complained.

"I don't want to hear it. Go grab your father and throw the football around so he doesn't get it in his head that he should come and help me with dinner."

"Aye aye, Captain!" I stood up from the stairs and saluted her before heading towards the family room off the back porch.

"Maybe Faith will be better in the kitchen than the two of you."

I stopped dead in my tracks and swiveled around to stare at my mom after what she'd said registered in my brain. "Faith?"

"Yes, I invited her to join us today."

"You invited her to Thanksgiving?" For as much as my mom loved to entertain, she'd always kept the major holidays to family only.

"I know," she sighed, offering me an apologetic

smile as she held her hands up in surrender. "It's horribly hypocritical of me to have invited her over when I'm the one who set the no guests rule, but I like to think you would have done the same thing if you'd heard her plans for the day."

"What was she going to do?"

"Stay on campus, eat in the cafeteria while it was open during the day, and microwave something later on! I couldn't let her do that, could I? Not on Thanksgiving."

"Of course you couldn't," I reassured, moving close enough to wrap her up in a hug.

"You're sure you don't mind?" she mumbled against my shirt.

I let her go and moved back so I could look down at her face. "Not even a little bit. If I wasn't such a dumbass, I would've thought to ask her about her plans and then I could've just asked her to come over myself."

The worry left my mom's eyes, only to be replaced by speculation. "Dumbass, huh?"

"Mom," I groaned, quickly regretting my choice of words because I knew what that look meant for me. She was going into matchmaker mode, which never seemed to go well for me. It should've been a good thing this time around since her sights were finally set on a girl I was actually interested in, but I wasn't sure how Faith would react to my mom's prodding. She was already hesitant enough as it was.

Our schedules had been at odds with each other over the past couple of weeks, and I hadn't seen her since I'd dropped her off at her dorm after we had dinner. We'd texted some and talked on the phone a few times, though. I felt like I was getting to know her, but slowly because she didn't seem big on letting people in. It made sense considering her background, but having my mom interfere could undo the small amount of progress I'd made with her.

"What? You could do a lot worse than Faith. She's beautiful, kind, smart, caring—"

"I know all that, Mom."

"Oh, you do?" She looked confused when I nodded. "Then what's the problem? Are you just not that into her?"

My head dropped and I stared at my feet, rubbing a hand over my head. "You really need to stop reading books, watching reality television, or whatever it was where you heard that saying."

She didn't seem bothered by my complaint. At all. She laughed before she raised her eyebrow and gestured with her hand in a circle that was probably intended to tell me to get on with it because she wasn't going to let me get away with not answering her question. "The problem is that I don't need my mom to help me get the girl I'm interested in. You're bound to do more harm than good since she's more skittish than that colt you and Dad bought when I was six."

Her brown eyes were hopeful as she stared up at me. "So what you're saying is that you're interested in Faith?"

Of course that was the part she zeroed in on. I hated admitting it to her because she was the most stubborn person I knew once she got something into her head, but there was no point denying the truth when it was already obvious what my answer was. "Yes."

"Okay, then I'll just have to trust you to do what you need to do to get the girl." I was mid-way through a sigh of relief when she added, "Unless I decide you need a little help."

"No help, Mom," I growled.

She gave me her patented puppy dog look; the one that always worked on my dad. "Not even a tiny bit?"

That look worked on me almost as well as my

dad, but I couldn't afford to fall for it this time. I knew if I didn't put my foot down now, she was going to have our wedding planned and Faith at the altar with a shotgun before I knew it. "Absolutely no help at all. Not even a tiny bit."

"Fine," she sighed. "I guess I'll have to be satisfied with getting her here so the two of you can spend your first holiday together."

It was so like her to point out that she'd already helped me with Faith in the hope that I'd back off and let her do it again. And although I was grateful for her interference in this one instance, I couldn't say so. It would only egg her on, and she didn't need any help with that. It didn't matter if I'd made it blatantly clear that I didn't want her help and she'd said she would leave it at what she'd already done, she couldn't stop there. "Maybe I should cancel the return trip for the car I hired so you can be the one to drop her off at campus instead."

"Car? What car? Why isn't she driving herself over?"

"Guys and their selective hearing," she sighed, shaking her head.

"Mom!" I snapped. "I don't need another lecture about listening. I need to know what you meant about Faith and the car."

"Okay. Okay." She held her hands up. "I'll explain it again since you obviously weren't paying close enough attention when I asked you to pick Faith up when the two of you went to her old high school a couple of weeks ago."

I was close to losing my patience, and my mom was enjoying every moment she could drag this out and torture me. It was payback for insisting she back off, most likely. "And?"

"She doesn't have a car, Dillon."

"Oh."

"Yeah, oh. Faith is a former foster kid. She doesn't have any family to help out. The only reason she's been able to attend Southeastern is because of the tuition waiver program she talks to all those high school students about. Your dumbass comment from earlier? It was more on the mark than I realized when it comes to Faith or else you would have already figured out that she can't afford to buy a car."

The implication behind her explanation rocked me. "Then how does she get to the schools she visits?"

"Some rideshare app on her phone, which is why I hired a car for her to use today, because I didn't feel right about having her accepting a ride from some random stranger to come over to our house. Not when I could send a town car instead."

"You've gotta be fucking kidding me."

"Language." My dad lightly smacked me on the backside of my head when he walked up behind me.

"It's not directed at me, honey," my mom reassured him.

"It better not be," he grumbled as he moved to her side and wrapped an arm around her shoulders, pulling her close like he always did whenever she was near.

"I think our boy finally met a girl who makes him feel all protective, like you are with me."

"Oh really?" My dad's grin matched my mom's when his attention switched back to me. "Who's the lucky girl?"

My mom answered for me. "Faith."

"The girl you've been working with on that project over at the college? The one with all the foster kids?"

"Yes, she's the one they wrote the newspaper article about because she started the whole thing."

"There's an article about her?" I asked, pulling my phone out of my pocket to look it up on the internet. "When?"

"About four months ago, right before the school year started."

"The same program you suggested Dillon could help with as part of our agreement with him after the black eye incident earlier this month?" My gaze jerked up from the screen of my phone to find my dad staring at my mom with narrowed eyes.

"Yes."

His head cocked to the side. "Started by the same girl you invited over to celebrate Thanksgiving with us?"

"Uh-huh."

"Elaine! Have you been planning this all along?"

She blinked her eyes in a gesture that was meant to make her look innocent but failed because we both knew her too well.

"How long, Mom?" I wouldn't put it past her if she'd been planning it from the moment she read the article about Faith.

"Since I met her for lunch," she admitted sheepishly. "What can I say? She was pretty, smart, and kind. Plus, we hit it off so well. I figured if there was a way for me to arrange for the two of you to meet, maybe I'd luck out."

"You're the worst," I chuckled, shaking my head.

"Or the best," she corrected as the doorbell rang. "Since there's your girl right now."

Damn. It was hard to disagree with her logic when she was right...something I should've learned by now since she liked to tell us she was always right.

Chapter Ten

FAITH

"Holy freaking hell," I mumbled under my breath, standing on what must have been the biggest porch in the history of the world. It wrapped around the front of an enormous brick house that was at the end of a long, winding driveway. There was a detached five-car garage off to the left of the house, in addition to the attached three-car one to the right.

I knew the Montgomerys had money, but I'd never imagined the kind of wealth it took to own a property like this. Not even with all Elaine had done for my group of students. Their house was more an estate than a home, with a perfectly cut lawn as far as the eye could see. And I was almost positive I'd seen horses out in the distance when we'd turned off from the road onto their driveway.

I'd been excited all morning about joining Elaine, her husband, and Dillon for the holiday. Then the town car had arrived to pick me up, and I was a little nervous along with a whole lot grateful for the ride because the drive was about thirty minutes and the car was incredibly comfortable. And free.

But now that I'd been dropped off on their doorstep, I was nervous as hell and wondering if I'd made the right decision when I'd accepted Elaine's invitation. But it was too late to change my mind since the car had already pulled around the circular drive and was on its way back to the road.

Then the door opened, and Dillon was standing in front of me with a welcoming smile. Staring up at him, I forgot why I'd started to second-guess myself in the first place.

"Hi." I added a quick wave with my free hand and clutched the container filled with cookies with the other as I held it out to him. "I brought some no-bake pumpkin cookies for dessert."

Dillon's eyes lit with humor, but not in a way that said he was making fun of my awkwardness. It was more like he appreciated it, as crazy as that was. "I wonder if I can sneak them past my mom and dad? I love all things pumpkin, and it'd be great if I could keep these all to myself."

Elaine swept past him, grabbing the container from Dillon's hands before she moved forward to wrap me up in a quick hug. "If anyone gets to hoard the pumpkin cookies, it's me. It's only right since I'm the one who invited Faith to join us today."

"Hey, no fair!" Dillon complained, trying to take the cookies back from his mom. It was hilarious watching her keep them away from him when he had about six inches and at least fifty pounds on her. There was no doubt he could've taken them from her if he'd wanted, but instead, he let her win the scuffle easily. I found it sweet; how Dillon was gentle with his mom.

It sent those butterflies swirling again, but in a different way than before. They weren't because of how hot he was; even though his short-sleeved shirt was tight and did amazing things for his chest, shoulders, and arms. This kind of butterfly was trickier than the ones caused by the chemistry between us. They couldn't be ignored quite as easily...because they were the first sign I was starting to develop feelings for him. Of course, I had to realize it right when I was standing in front of his parents.

And it was the first time I met his father. Because that was just my luck.

At least I was good at shoving my feelings into a box and storing them away for later...or never. Because the habit came in handy when Dillon's dad stepped around his wife and son and held his hand out to me.

"Ignore them. I do it all the time when they're like this," he suggested as we shook hands.

"Hey!" Elaine cried, sounding exactly like her son had just moments ago.

Her husband flashed her a playful grin that reminded me of Dillon's smile. "You know it's true."

"Yes, but you don't need to tell everyone about it," she chided.

"But Faith isn't just anyone. I've been hearing about her from you since August." He turned his grin on me. "And then there's Dil—"

A gasp burst from my throat when Elaine slapped her hand over his mouth. It turned into a giggle when Dillon tugged on my hand to lead me past his parents, saying, "My dad is the one who had it wrong. They're the ones you should ignore when they're acting like this, which is pretty much all of the time."

I thought they *all* had it wrong. The way

Dillon's family interacted with each other was special, and nobody should ignore that kind of beauty. Ever.

"I actually kind of like it."

"You do, huh?"

"Yeah, it's nice to spend time with a family who's so happy together." My gaze swept across the foyer and into the living room, taking in all of the autumn-themed decorations. "To celebrate a holiday that's all about giving thanks when I actually have a decent-sized list of things for which I'm grateful."

"That's such a sweet thing to say." Elaine squeezed my shoulder as they joined us.

"We're happy to have you with us," his dad said.

"Thank you, Mr. Montgomery."

"Call me Lloyd, please."

I hadn't hesitated when I'd met Elaine and she'd told me the same thing. His request wasn't any different—it even made more sense for him to make the offer because I wasn't a complete stranger to him like I'd been with Elaine back when we'd had lunch in August. I was friends with his wife. I was...whatever word someone would use to describe what was happening between Dillon and me.

But it didn't feel as natural using Mr. Montgomery's first name. Probably because I'd never had any positive male role models in my life, except for the doctors who'd saved it. So I paused for what felt like a moment too long before replying, "Thank you, Lloyd."

Dillon stepped closer, his hand going to the small of my back. I took comfort in the gesture. Settled into his touch. Appreciated how he must've made the move because he'd sensed my discomfort and wanted to do something to ease it.

Elaine smiled, her eyes darting down to the small amount of space between us. "Why don't you give Faith a little tour while your dad and I go check on how dinner is doing in the kitchen?"

I felt the muscles in Dillon's arm tense and turned to look up at him. His dark eyes were wide, and he was shaking his head. "Do you think that's a good idea? Because I don't."

"You set fire to one turkey, and they judge your cooking skills forever," Lloyd muttered, tugging on Elaine's hand as they walked away.

"Do you like Chinese?" Dillon asked oddly.

"I heard that!" Lloyd yelled, making Elaine giggle.

"I feel like I missed something." I cocked my head to the side, giving Dillon a questioning look that wrinkled my brow. "Your dad set fire to a turkey?"

"And a big section of the backyard," he laughed. "C'mon, I'll start the tour there so I can show you."

He kept his hand on my back while he guided me through several rooms and led me through a set of French doors which opened to a stone paved patio that was even bigger than the front porch. We walked to the top of the steps that led down to the lawn, and Dillon pointed to the left. "Do you see the line in the grass there? Where the green changes to a slightly lighter shade?"

I held a hand to my forehead to block the glare from the sun and narrowed my eyes while I focused on the area he was pointing at. "Maybe?"

"It's hard to spot because my dad had the landscapers change out the sod three times until they got as close a match as possible," he explained.

"Your dad set fire to a turkey…on the lawn?" I still felt like I was missing a big part of the story.

"Yup. It was a deep-fried turkey disaster."

"Oh!" I nodded. "That actually makes sense. I've never had deep-fried turkey before, but I could see how something could go wrong with all that hot oil."

"Especially when my dad's the one doing the cooking," Dillon laughed. His hand slid from the small of my back to grab my hand. His fingers laced through mine, and he tugged me back into the house. "My mom never lets him help in the kitchen."

"And yet she let him use a deep fryer on the lawn to cook the Thanksgiving turkey?"

"Yup." He stopped in front of a stone fireplace and pointed at one of the photos on the mantle. It was of his parents on their wedding day, staring into each other's eyes as though they were the only two people in the world. "She loves him too much to say no when he really wants something, and he was dying to fry that turkey."

"That's"—I swallowed down a lump in my throat while I tried to find the perfect word—"incredible."

"I'll deny it if you tell them I said this, but I have to agree. My parents are definitely incredible."

"I'll keep your secret," I promised as I took in the rest of the pictures on the mantle. It took a moment before it registered that I was seeing double. Literally. "Wait. You have a twin?"

Dillon's fingers tightened around mine. "I did."

"Did?" I tore my gaze away from the photos of Dillon with a mirror image of himself and found him staring at the one of them standing side-by-side in football uniforms. He was holding perfectly still, the muscle in his jaw jumping and his eyes filled with despair.

"That car accident I was in my senior year? The one that landed me in the hospital? He died in the crash. On impact, but at least that means he didn't suffer, right?"

Oh, shit. No wonder Elaine had sounded like she was about to cry when we'd talked about Dillon's problems. She'd lost a son.

Dillon's brother.

Even worse...his identical twin.

I'd been a total bitch, judging him the way I initially had. Without bothering to look for what lay beneath the surface of his seemingly perfect life. If it had cost me the chance to stand by his side while he told me his story, I never would have known what I was missing. Even though I was starting to wonder if I would've felt the loss anyway.

"I'm sorry. I didn't know." The words sounded hollow, just like they did whenever anyone said them to me about my past. But I meant them. So very much. And I hoped he heard the sincerity in my voice.

He looked away from the photo and sighed. "We don't talk about him often. Even though it's been a few years, the loss is still too fresh. It hurts so fucking much."

"I can't even imagine."

"But you can," he disagreed. "I think that's part of it."

"Part of what?"

"Why the pull between us is so damn strong." I gasped at his admission, and he tugged me closer with a determined gleam in his eyes. "Don't even try to pretend it doesn't exist, Faith. Not when we're both feeling it. And definitely not when you're the first person I've opened up to about Declan."

"I—"

Shit. He was right. I couldn't deny it. Not in a moment where it felt like he was baring his soul to me. The least I could do was be honest with him and own up to the fact that I was starting to have feelings for him. "Yes, I feel it too."

"You climbed into my SUV, and it was like I'd been hit by a lightning bolt." His hand slid around my back to rest just above the swell of my ass. "You haven't told me much about your childhood, but I figured you had to have experienced your own loss if you ended up in foster care."

"My mom. When I was twelve." My gaze slid up to the picture of Dillon and his brother, their arms slung over each other's shoulders with huge grins on their identical faces. "But it wasn't much of a loss because she wasn't much of a mother to me in the first place."

Dillon's gaze followed mine. "Declan and I were identical in looks, but he was my better half in so many ways. He always got straight A's, without really trying. Didn't break any rules. No drinking, not even when we were at parties. He never tried smoking pot because he didn't want to risk getting kicked off the football team. He played first line for offense and defense."

About halfway through his recitation about his brother, I shifted my focus from the photos to Dillon's face. His despair was etched there, in the lines bracketing his mouth and the pallor in his complexion. "He sounds amazing."

"Declan was the best."

My eyes filled with tears at how profound his loss had been. I sniffled, drawing Dillon's attention away from the mantle.

"Look at my tough girl, crying for me." He lifted the hand at his side to swipe at my cheeks while the other pressed me closer to his body.

"Don't expect to see it again any time soon," I warned. "The last time I cried was almost four years ago when I found out I was getting a new kidney."

"Four years ago, this coming February," he

murmured. "That's the last time I cried; when I woke up from a four-week coma and found out Declan had died in the accident."

Whoa. Talk about a major coincidence. Four years ago, this coming February, was when I had my transplant.

Chapter Eleven

FAITH

"February seventh," I whispered. "That's when I got my new kidney. It was the best day of my life."

"The crash happened on January tenth, but I didn't wake up until the day after you had your transplant." His thumb swept across my cheek, and I shivered. "It was the worst moment of my life because that's when my parents told me Declan had died. I'd missed his funeral and was stuck in a hospital bed, unable to believe he was really gone. Not until I was discharged, and they took me to his grave. That's when it hit me. I'd spent my entire life, even before I was born, with Declan by my side...but he was gone, and I had to figure out how to move on by myself."

I tilted my head to the side and rubbed my cheek against his palm. "I'm so sorry."

"Thanks." Dillon offered me a sad smile. "It's kind of crazy to think we were both in the hospital at the same time, even though I was in a coma for most of my time there."

I did a quick calculation in my head. "I left six days after you woke up."

"I was at Southeast Memorial. You?"

"Yeah. Me, too." Same hospital. Same time frame. "It's such a small world."

"Full of coincidences that led you here." His head dipped lower. "To me."

"When you put it like that, it kinda seems like we were meant to meet."

He brushed his lips against mine. The gesture was gentle, our mouths barely touching. But it was still a kiss. And our first. I had no doubt it was a memory I'd never forget.

"More proof of that bond pulling us together," he murmured against my lips.

The way we fit didn't make any sense. It was too much. It was way too soon. But it felt real. And good. So I rose up on my toes and pressed my mouth against his to claim a second kiss. A longer and deeper one than the first.

It lasted until his mom called out and we

jumped apart from each other. "Dillon! You'd better get your dad out of the kitchen, or we're never going to eat!"

"She's not kidding," he chuckled. "I better get in there. You up for throwing the football a little bit with my dad and me?"

It wasn't at the top of my list of things to do since I was the furthest thing from athletic, but I wasn't going to say no to the offer. Not when it meant I got to spend time with Dillon, doing something that made him happy. "Sure. Sounds good to me."

"C'mon." He dropped another quick kiss on my lips before tugging on my hand to lead me into the kitchen. We stopped on the way to grab a football out of a closet off the hallway leading to the back of the house.

"Oh! You don't have to head out there with the boys, Faith. You're welcome to stay in here and help me instead," Elaine offered.

"You trying to steal my girl, Mom?"

My cheeks filled with heat at Dillon calling me his girl. It only deepened when Elaine and Lloyd's gazes dropped down to our hands, where our fingers were laced together. A huge grin split Elaine's face, and Lloyd chuckled as he kissed her cheek.

"Maybe you should've let me be your helper, and then we wouldn't have interrupted the kids."

"Except then we wouldn't have any dinner to eat because you would have found a way to ruin it all," she teased.

"We could've had Chinese again." He jumped out of the way when she picked up a towel from the counter and snapped it at him. "Okay. Okay. We're going."

Dillon opened the sliding glass door that led to the other side of the stone patio we'd been on earlier. As we walked outside, I heard Elaine mutter something along the lines of Chinese food being a worthy sacrifice. I wasn't sure what she meant by that, but Dillon and Lloyd seemed to understand because they both burst into fits of laughter that lasted until we'd made it all the way down to the grass. Lloyd headed to the left, and Dillon and I went to the right.

"What'd I miss?" I asked Dillon when we were about fifty feet away from his dad.

"Thanksgiving dinner is my mom's and my absolute favorite meal. We love all of it. The turkey, mashed potatoes with gravy, stuffing, cranberries, rolls, and pumpkin pie." He flashed me an approving grin. "We both also love anything pumpkin flavored, so the cookies you made were the perfect thing to bring."

"You haven't even tried them yet," I reminded him. "They could be awful."

"They're pumpkin flavored, and you made them for me." He paused to throw the ball to his dad in a perfect spiral. "So I'm going to love them."

"I actually made them for your mom since she's the one who invited me." His dad threw the ball our way, and Dillon caught it and tossed it back before reacting to my joke. Then he wrapped his arms around my torso and lifted me off my feet, twirling me around until I got dizzy. "Dillon!"

"What?" he asked after setting me back on the grass.

I clutched onto his arms to steady myself. "I was just teasing."

"Pumpkin cookies are nothing to joke about. Not with me or my mom."

"You guys sure are serious about your Thanksgiving meal," I muttered as he caught the ball and threw it back to his dad again.

"That's putting it mildly," he laughed. "My mom's love for turkey dinner is a sure sign of how happy my mom is about us being a couple. If I hadn't already realized you had her stamp of approval before you got here, that would've clinched it."

A couple? Stamp of approval? So much about his statement blew my mind, making me dizzier than the twirling had just moments ago. "What do you mean?"

"That comment, about Chinese food being worth the sacrifice?"

"Yeah?"

I wanted to stomp my foot when he paused again to catch the ball. "You want to throw it this time?"

"No, what I want is for you to explain about the Chinese food thing."

He seemed to find my frustration amusing because he laughed while tossing the ball back to his dad.

"Dillon," I growled.

"You're cute when you're irritated. Did you know that? I noticed it the first time we met." I glared at him, making him laugh again before he finally answered, "My mom would've been willing to eat Chinese today, sacrificing her favorite meal, if it brought the two of us together."

"Shut up! Really?" My gaze slid to the house, where I could see through the windows to where she was working in the kitchen. I respected Elaine a hell of a lot. It wasn't just because of what she'd done for the foster kids at my school, either—although that would have been enough of a reason. But she was a genuinely nice person who cared about others and didn't have a problem showing it. I hadn't known a lot of people like Elaine in my life, and it made me appreciate those qualities in her more.

"Yeah, really. It's why she tried so hard to make sure we met." Dillon caught the ball again and nodded when his dad said he was going inside to check to see how much longer it'd be before Elaine needed help setting the table. "See, even Dad is in on it now that he knows what my mom was trying to do."

It was hard for me to believe that Elaine was trying to pair me off with her son. At least she'd gotten to know me, so it wasn't entirely out of the realm of possibility. But Dillon's dad? We'd just met today. I couldn't imagine how much Elaine had to have raved about me for him to be okay with his son dating a foster kid with nothing to her name. "Maybe he's just really excited about dinner."

"No, I don't think so." He tossed the ball at the bottom of the steps leading up the stone patio and gripped both of my hands once his were free. "My dad's a sharp guy. He probably clocked our body language the whole time we were out here and decided we could do with a little bit of alone time before dinner is ready."

"What? No!" My eyes went wide, and my cheeks filled with heat. "Do you really think so?"

"Is it so hard to believe?"

"But he's your dad." My voice dropped a notch, like they could hear me from inside the house.

"Yeah, but it's not like we're teenagers who need a chaperone twenty-four seven." He yanked me closer. "Or that we could get into too much trouble out here anyway."

"This is so weird."

"Which part?"

"All of it!" I felt his chest shake with laughter and nudged him in the shin with my shoe.

"Ouch!" He gave me an exaggerated wince.

"Oh, please," I snorted. "I barely touched you."

"I already told you how much I like it when you're irritated." His eyes were filled with humor, but they also held a thread of heat. "If you keep it up, I'll be tempted to put the time my dad gave us to good use."

And if they hadn't been inside with a clear view of us, I might've been coaxed into finding out exactly how we would've passed that time. It was crazy! The pull between us was strong enough to get me to act completely out of character. It was turning me boy crazy for the first time in my life—but only when it came to one, specific guy. Dillon Montgomery...who was grinning down at me and making those butterflies take flight yet again.

"You're impossible."

The heat in his eyes ratcheted up a notch. "Impossibly attracted to you."

"You're quick with the perfect lines, slick." Really damn smooth while I still felt awkward and nervous around him. It was understandable since I didn't have much dating experience. Seeing my mom with so many strange men when I was young had given me a skewed perspective on romantic relationships. Coupled with my not-so-great experiences in foster care, my illness, and the scars from my transplant, and I'd gotten in the habit of avoiding potential relationships for the most part. But Dillon had snuck in there; tricking me into our first date. Blindsiding me by calling us a couple. Making me feel things I didn't expect. "Should I be worried?"

"If what I'm saying is coming off as perfect, that's just blind luck." He shook his head and let go of one of my hands to run his through his hair. "I'm flying blind here, Faith."

"It doesn't seem like it from where I'm standing." I took a couple of steps backwards, and his hold on my hand tightened.

"I dated some in high school, but nothing too serious. Then Declan died, and everything changed. *I* changed," he stressed, the words practically ripped from his chest. "I was messed up in the head for a long time, struggling with guilt because the one thing I was better at than him was driving. I couldn't get it out of my head that if I'd been behind the wheel instead of him, maybe the accident wouldn't have happened. But I'd had a few drinks and a hit from a bong at the party we'd gone to, so Declan took my keys."

His confession ripped my heart to shreds, and I closed the distance I'd put between us. "You know it wasn't your fault, though. Right?"

"Most days, yeah. And on the others, I turn to gambling. It's been my outlet for the past few years because I couldn't stand the thought of drinking or smoking pot after Declan died. Or dating."

He was hot. Rich. A good guy. Even though he was a little messed up, understandably so with what happened to his twin, Dillon Montgomery was one hell of a catch. Most of the girls on campus had to have been chasing after him on the regular. "No dating?"

"Nothing serious. A few hookups the summer

before my freshman year before I realized they just made me feel worse. I just ended up at an underground poker game afterwards. It fucked with my head, and I lost each time. I finally figured out that casual shit wasn't for me, but a serious relationship wasn't either." He shrugged. "It would've meant opening up to a girl about Declan, and I couldn't wrap my head around the idea of doing that."

"But you told me?" It put our conversation in front of the fireplace into a whole new perspective.

"Sharing with you felt right."

He sounded more okay with that than I was. "Because you think of us as a couple?"

"Yup."

"Even though we've only been on one date?"

"What can I say? When you know, you know." He grinned and winked at me. "I never understood what my dad meant when he told me that, but now I get it."

I'd seen how his dad was with Elaine and caught the implication. As shocking as it was. Thrilling. And scary, too. Some of what I was feeling must have shown on my face because he hurriedly urged, "Don't be afraid to let me in. Share as much or as little as you'd like. I know we haven't known each other long, but I'd destroy anyone who tried to hurt you."

His eyes gleamed with sincerity. Knowing he'd made himself vulnerable with me left me in the unusual position of being open to the idea of doing the same. "I'll try."

"I appreciate it." He lowered his head and pressed his lips against mine in a kiss that was gentle and...meaningful. When his dad opened the sliding door to call out for us to come inside, it ended too soon. "You just gave me the best reason to be thankful on my favorite holiday."

I had a big smile on my face when I walked with him into the house. Then I enjoyed the best Thanksgiving meal I'd ever had, surrounded by amazing people and filled with gratitude because maybe—just maybe—I'd finally found my path to happiness.

Chapter Twelve

FAITH

Discovering what it meant to be in a relationship with Dillon over the next few weeks was fun. Exciting. More interesting than I expected.

Both of us had busy schedules. Classes. My volunteer work. His internship at his dad's company. But we still made time for each other. Dinners out. Movies. Bowling. Mini golf. Ice skating. Study sessions.

We did all the traditional stuff, but Dillon also got creative with a few of his date ideas. For one of our dinner dates, we went to three different restaurants. A tapas place for appetizers, pho for entrées, and French for dessert. It was like an international food tour, and one of the best meals I'd ever had.

Second only to the turkey and sides Elaine had made on Thanksgiving.

Another time, we drove almost an hour away to go to a pickle festival. I hadn't even known pickle festivals existed, but Dillon had somehow managed to find one because he thought I'd enjoy it. When we'd had lunch on campus together a few days earlier, I'd stolen Dillon's pickle off his plate. I loved them, but I never let the cafeteria staff put one on mine because they were so high in sodium and I had zero willpower when it came to their salty deliciousness. I enjoyed the hell out of the one I snagged from Dillon, though. A little bit too much because it'd inspired him to make some jokes about it all day. Sexual ones, of course. He was a guy, after all. We had such a good time at the festival, those jokes actually sounded kinda funny by the end of the day.

We'd also gone to the zoo, a trivia night at a local bar, and a wine tasting. It'd gotten to the point where I never knew what to expect from him, but I never doubted I'd enjoy whatever Dillon had come up with.

"What're you and the hottie doing tonight?" Christine, my roommate since our freshman year, was lying on her stomach on her bed. She had a spiral notebook, a variety of highlighters and pens, two textbooks, and her cell phone spread out in front of her.

"No idea." I finished tying my laces and wiggled my feet before getting up. "He only told me to wear comfortable shoes."

"He likes to keep you guessing, doesn't he?"

"Which amuses you to no end."

"You can't really blame me for that," she laughed. "Not when I'm having a blast watching you leave your comfort zone without a single complaint. I've tried for years to get you to loosen up and have some fun, but you always had a perfectly good explanation for why you couldn't come out with me. Your health. A paper you had to write. A test you needed to study for. A high school visit that you needed to wake up for super early the next morning."

When she listed my reasons out that way, it sounded like I'd been trying to avoid spending time with her. But that hadn't been my intention. Not at all. Christine was the closest thing I'd ever had to a best friend, and I was a total asshat for not taking the time to hang out with her more often over the years—even if the parties she liked to go to weren't my thing. "You know they weren't excuses, right? I wasn't trying to avoid spending time with you or anything like that."

"I know," she reassured me. "And I understand, Faith. When they paired us up as roommates, we were strangers whose only connection was the time we spent in the system. But I've gotten to know you pretty well over the past few years, and I didn't take it personally that you weren't into the same things I was."

That was a huge relief, but not much of a surprise since Christine was much easier going than I was. "I'm glad because I'd hate for you to think that I don't consider you my friend."

"Of course you do." She rolled her blue eyes and laughed, tossing her long, blonde hair over one shoulder. "You never would have agreed to live with me for three more years if you didn't secretly love me."

"Yup. Total girl crush. It's why I had to limit how much time I spent in your presence. So I didn't fall totally in love with you," I deadpanned.

"I totally get it. I mean"—she fluttered her eyelashes—"everyone can't be as awesome as me. Right?"

"Yeah," I snorted. "That's exactly what I like best about you. Your awesomeness."

"Better not let your hottie hear you say that. He might get jealous of how into me you really are."

It was so wrong of me, but I couldn't help

smiling a little bit because she was right. *Ish.* Dillon wasn't a crazy jealous person who resented my roommate, but he had a thing about other guys looking at me. He swore it happened all the time, but I figured it was just a convenient excuse for all the public displays of affection because I rarely noticed guys checking me out.

"Don't fool yourself into thinking I don't see that smug little grin of yours and know exactly what's behind it," she teased.

"But can you blame me for it?"

"Not even a tiny bit," she giggled. "Your man is totally into you, and he's hot with a capital H."

"He's also going to be here any minute." I went over to my desk and checked my purse to make sure I had money and my ID. After a quick search through the contents, I dropped my phone inside and headed for the door.

"Faith?" I opened it before I looked back at Christine. "Seriously, we all have damage from our pasts. Part of yours was that it was hard for you to let go and just have fun. But it made sense. You were focused on doing the right thing because you felt like you had a debt to pay because of your kidney."

She was right. In some ways, I still did. But then I reminded myself of what Dr. Stewart had told me about living my life to the fullest and honoring their gift by being happy. I gave her a jerky nod as I opened the door.

"I can't tell you how happy I am that you aren't letting any of that get in the way of you spending time with your hottie now."

"Me, too." My reply was muffled by the shutting of the door behind me, but it was heartfelt. I was grateful to the magnetic pull I felt towards Dillon because it'd shaken me up. Taken me out of my comfort zone and into an unknown that was better than I could have possibly dreamed.

For someone who hadn't been in a relationship since high school, Dillon was the perfect boyfriend. At least for me. He was attentive, sending me texts when we were apart and calling me on the nights we didn't get together. He was observant too, noticing my likes and dislikes and taking them into consideration when he made plans. Even with the little stuff, like grabbing an extra bottle of water whenever we had lunch together and telling me to take it with me to my next class. Or keeping healthy snacks in the fridge at his place for when we hung out over there.

It all settled me. Quieted the tiny voice inside my head that tried to convince me nothing was permanent, and nobody stuck around. Dillon battled my doubts each and every day, and he won without even knowing he was fighting against them.

Because he was just that good to me.

Because we fit together.

Like he and his dad liked to put it, 'when you know, you know.' And my head was starting to believe what my heart felt like it knew with Dillon—we were supposed to be together.

With that thought in my head, I rushed forward when I saw his SUV at the curb in front of my dorm. The windows were rolled down, and I smiled when the usual butterflies swirled in my belly at the sight of him in the driver's seat. As I climbed inside, his dark eyes swept over my tight jeans and slouchy top, filling with heat at my choice of outfit for today's date.

"How is it that you manage to look perfect when you don't even know where I'm taking you?"

"Lucky guesses?"

I buckled my seat belt, and he leaned over to claim my lips in a quick kiss that left me breathless for more.

"Or maybe you just know me better than you realize," he suggested, giving me another kiss before pulling away from the curb and heading off campus.

"But not well enough to ever figure out where

you're taking me before we get there. You do too good of a job at coming up with ideas I'd never think to guess."

"You don't give your own creativity enough credit. You're the one who found that outdoor movie we went to a couple of weeks ago."

"True," I conceded. It was one of the few times he'd let me do the planning. And I'd had to think way outside the box on that one because he didn't like me spending money when we were together. But I was determined to treat him to a night out, so I'd scoured the internet for ideas until I discovered that a nearby park did free movies on Friday nights. Everyone brought their own blankets and lawn chairs to sit out on the lawn, and there was an ice cream truck that came by with treats. I'd packed us popcorn, candy, and drinks and we'd cuddled on a blanket surrounded by families with kids while we watched an animated movie. It had been awesome, and we planned to go again sometime soon.

"But that doesn't mean I'm not dying to know what we're doing tonight."

"How about I give you a hint?"

He flashed me a grin that made me think his hint wouldn't do me much good, but I still took him up on the offer. "Yes, please."

"Chocolate, strawberry, and vanilla."

There was only one guess for that hint. "Ice cream!"

"Yup."

"Are we going out for ice cream?"

"Not exactly."

"I knew it couldn't be that easy," I grumbled.

"But only because surprising you is so much fun."

It really was, so I didn't complain too much for the ten minutes we were in the car before arriving at a local cooking school.

"Are we going to make our own ice cream?" The awe in my voice made me sound like a little girl who'd just seen Santa for the first time.

"Yeah, my mom had a flyer for this place because she's taken a few classes here. When I noticed they were focusing on ice cream tonight, I signed us up."

"I love ice cream." More than loved it. I could've happily eaten ice cream at every meal if it wasn't so unhealthy. "But I've never made it before."

"Neither have I, but they're going to do a couple of low-ingredient, all-natural recipes that you can eat as often as you'd like because they aren't that bad for you."

I'd known he was considerate, but the thought

he'd put into this plan blew me away. It wasn't just about taking me to make something I loved for the first time. He'd found a way for me to indulge my ice cream addiction without having to worry. "Dillon," I whispered, my voice shaking.

"Shit." He parked the car and turned to face me, worry etched on his handsome face. "You hate the idea, don't you? Fuck, I'm sorry. I thought you'd love it."

"How long do we have before the class starts?"

"What?" His gaze slid to the clock on his dash. "Fifteen minutes, but we can skip it and grab dinner instead."

I shook my head as I unbuckled my seat belt and dropped my purse at my feet. Then I climbed over the console onto his lap. "Push your seat all the way back, honey."

"Holy fuck." He hit a button, and his seat slid back. It gave me enough space to settle on his lap, and his hard length pressed against my core. "What're you doing, baby?"

"Just saying thank you for being so incredible to me." I wrapped my arms around his neck and brushed my lips against his.

"We're in a public parking lot, Faith." His gaze swept out the window to scan the parking lot.

"I'm not going to do anything we could get into

trouble for," I whispered against his ear. I nipped at the lobe softly, and he groaned.

"Didn't pick something you'd like because I wanted you to feel like you owe me anything. I'm not in a rush, Faith. As badly as I want you"—his hips jerked forward to show me just how much—"which is a fucking lot, I'll wait as long as it takes for you to be ready for that step. There's no pressure here. We have all the time in the world."

"I know we do." I smiled down at him. "And I'm going to spend the next fifteen minutes of it making out with my boyfriend."

With our mouths pressed together, tongues tangled, and hands stroking over our clothes, we lost track of time. It ended up being more like twenty minutes...and the only reason we made it inside for the class at all was because someone tapped on the fogged up windows and told us to knock it off. Learning how to make homemade ice cream and a steamy make-out session. Best date ever.

Chapter Thirteen

DILLON

The last few Christmases had been difficult for me. It'd been Declan's favorite time of the year—the entire two weeks we got off school for winter break. He'd been like a little kid jazzed up on caffeine and sugar for sixteen days straight. So many of my best memories of him were from over the holidays. Other than the anniversary of the crash, it was when I felt his loss the most. It felt like forever since I'd been able to get into the Christmas mood.

This year was different because it was my first with Faith, and I was determined to make it special for her. She deserved the best, but she'd never really gotten it before. No mounds of presents under a big Christmas tree when she was little. Hell, she'd been lucky to get a tree at all, let alone gifts. I wanted her to have it all, and I went a little overboard organizing it.

Between ordering a tree, picking out decorations, buying presents, and pestering my mom to bake a bunch of cookies, I channeled some serious holiday spirit. There had even been one moment when I'd been decorating the tree when I thought to myself that Declan would've been proud. It was the first time since he'd died that I'd been able to think about him at Christmas time without wanting to gamble. Faith had given that to me, and it was better than any gift money could buy.

It made everything I'd pulled together for our first holiday as a couple pale in comparison.

Corey, my best friend and partner in crime for the past few years, didn't seem to agree. "Dude. It looks like Christmas threw up in here. Are you sure you don't want to pull down some of this shit before Faith gets here and clues into the fact that she's dating an insane person?"

I shoved my elbow into his side. "Fuck off."

"You better be careful or else that's going to be the last thing you say to me before I leave your ass and head to Europe."

"I still can't believe you picked this semester to

study in Italy and fucked up your graduation plans."

He swept his arm in an arc. "At least I'll be able to escape the Winter Wonderland you set up in our living room."

"*Our?*" I quirked an eyebrow at him.

"Hey! I've lived here ever since your parents bought the place. That makes it mine as much as yours, right?"

"I don't think that's how it works, man."

He shrugged his shoulders. "Eh, it was worth a shot."

"But I'll let you lay claim to your bedroom if you want. It'll still be here if you hate Italy and want to come back early."

"Hate Italy?" He reared back in feigned shock. "I was only kinda joking when I said Faith was dating an insane person, but now I realize how right I was. A whole country full of hot babes with sexy accents? What's not to love?"

Coming from any other guy, I would've believed it. But Corey had gone through a rough breakup over the summer and hadn't dated anyone else since then. When he'd told me about the semester in Italy, I'd wondered if he was doing it to put half the world between him and his ex. He seemed excited, and I hadn't wanted to ruin it for him so I kept my trap shut. But I still wanted him to know I had his back, even if half the world separated us too.

"Well, if you decide boring American accents are more your thing, the offer still stands."

"Thanks, man. I appreciate it." He slapped me on the back before picking up his backpack and rolling his suitcase to the door. "But if the impossible somehow happens, I'll call first because I'd hate to come back and find out you've replaced me with a new roomie."

"Do you really think I'm going to replace you?"

"With your hot-as-fuck girlfriend? Hell yeah, I do!"

"Dude," I chuckled, shaking my head. "It's been like six weeks. She's not moving in any time soon."

He swung the door open and turned his head to look at me over his shoulder. "I'm gonna remind you that you said that when I get back and you two are living together."

I laughed it off at the time, but Corey's parting words were all I thought about for the next two days. To the point where I almost convinced myself to wrap a spare key and put it under the tree for Faith as an extra present. But then I came to my senses. I figured if she wasn't comfortable enough with me yet to have sex, then she would freak the fuck out if I asked her to move in with me. So when she came over on Christmas Eve—since I'd convinced my parents to settle for us coming over on Christmas morning—there weren't any gifts for her to open that would send her running.

Everything else was as perfect as I could make it when I opened the door to her. Holiday music was playing through the sound system. The lights on the tree were lit. Christmas cookies were spread out on the kitchen counter. And I had eggnog spiked with bourbon in the fridge. It wasn't a favorite of mine, but I had to get it because Faith had somehow never tried it before. "Ho ho ho."

"Well, hello there." Her entire face lit up with pleasure when she saw the Santa hat on my head. It had a sprig of mistletoe hanging from a ball on the end. "Is that a hint that I'm supposed to kiss Santa?"

"Definitely."

"Earn your kiss." She shoved a big, rectangular-shaped present into my hands. "By putting this under the tree for me."

"For me?"

"Yup."

"Maybe we should do presents first. Since I'm not sure I can handle the torture of wondering what's under this wrapping paper." I gave the package a little shake as I walked over to the tree, but it didn't make any rattling noises. When I turned back around, Faith was standing just inside the door, laughing her ass off. "What?"

"I'm going to have to tell Christine to change your nickname from 'hottie' to 'Mr. Hypocritical' since you get so much enjoyment out of keeping our plans a secret for most of our dates."

"Hottie, huh?" I flashed her a grin. "I'd hate to give up such a great nickname.

"It would be a shame," she agreed.

"But it's not just that I'm dying to know what you picked out for me. It's also that I'd like to give you at least one of your presents now so we can use it later."

"Fine. Twist my arm and make me open a present," she sighed before moving into the living room and twirling around to take in all of the decorations I'd put up. "Holy shit. Please tell me you didn't get me anything else because this"—she did another slow circle—"is the perfect gift."

"I hate to disappoint." I didn't sound even the tiniest bit sincere since I didn't mean it. "But plenty of those presents under the tree are for you."

"What? No!" she gasped, going over to the tree and dropping to her knees. "You went overboard. It's too much. Way, way too much."

"Most of them are random, small things so you

have stuff to unwrap in the morning." Since we were heading over to my parents' for breakfast, she'd agreed to spend the night at my place. For the first time. "But your real gift is what I want you to open now."

"I guess we could each open one present now, and save the others for tomorrow."

I didn't give her the chance to second-guess her agreement and moved to her side. I pulled the biggest present out from under the tree and set it in front of her. "Open this one."

She ripped into the wrapping paper and gasped when she saw what was inside. "An ice cream maker?"

"Yup, I thought we could make pumpkin ice cream for later."

"Pumpkin, huh?" she laughed. "I guess I won't feel bad about the extra presents in the morning since I have a couple more for you too, and it seems my big present is as much for you as it is for me."

"I bought the ingredients for chocolate, strawberry, and vanilla, too."

"The same flavors from our ice cream making date," she whispered, leaning into me and sliding her hand around the base of my skull to tug my face towards hers. When she pressed her lips against mine, I forgot all about the presents until she pulled away from me and handed me the rectangular package she'd had me put under the tree.

"Shopping for the guy who has everything and is so damn thoughtful that you want to give him the perfect gift because you know that's what he's going to get you is hard."

I pressed a fingertip against her lips to stop her rambling. "I'm sure I'll love it. Whatever it is. Because it's from you."

"And you clearly have excellent taste since you picked me."

She narrowed her pretty brown eyes at me. "Stop being so cute while I'm super nervous about how you're going to react to what I got you."

"There's only one way to fix that." I tore the paper off my present, revealing a piece of artwork in shades of blue. It was a bit obscure, with vertical lines that had horizontal bars in staggered spots inside them. "It's cool."

"Remember when I asked you to do that cheek swab for my friend who was doing a research project on the efficacy of those ancestry websites?"

"Yeah." It'd been an odd request, but I'd had people ask stranger things of me on campus.

"I lied. It wasn't for a friend's project," she admitted, pointing at the blue lines. "It was for this; an artistic rendering of your DNA."

"My DNA?"

"Yours." She took a deep breath before she continued, "And Declan's."

I looked at the painting in stunned shock, reaching out to trace the lines with a trembling hand. "I didn't know anything like this existed. I can't believe you bought this for me."

"Do you like it?"

I set the painting to the side and pulled Faith into my arms. "I fucking love it, baby."

There weren't enough words to explain to her how much her gift meant to me, so I showed her instead. I consumed her lips in a deep kiss, her soft curves molded against my chest. Her lips clung to mine, and she made a soft purring sound deep in her throat. I knew I needed to rein it in and pull away from her, but I couldn't bring myself to do it. Not when my defenses were down because she'd blown them away with her gift.

Chapter Fourteen

FAITH

Dillon and I had kissed many times before, but it'd never felt quite like it did right then. He sparked emotions in me that I wasn't certain how to deal with, but I knew I wanted to keep feeling them. And I didn't want to hold back any longer. Not when we were alone in front of the prettiest Christmas tree I'd ever seen with the lights twinkling around us. After weeks of flirting, kissing, and making out, things were about to get real.

When I kicked my shoes off, Dillon followed suit and removed his too without breaking eye contact with me. Lifting my shirt and raising it over my head, I was anxious about getting topless with a guy...until he repeated the gesture. At that point, his naked chest and rippling muscles distracted me from my nervousness.

"I've wanted to see you with your shirt off ever since I saw you playing football in the quad my freshman year," I whispered. "I could barely tear my eyes away from you to watch where I was walking."

"I wish you'd have come up to me and introduced yourself back then."

"Ummmm, no way." I was still adjusting to life post-transplant and hadn't been ready for him, but the timing was right for us now.

"I tend to forget that my tough girl is shy. Thank fuck I found you," he rasped. "Because you can see me like this whenever you'd like. And touch me, baby. Any time. Anywhere. If you want me, then I'm all yours."

I ran my fingertips along his warm skin, pressing a kiss to the long scar that ran down the left side of his rib cage and tracing the muscles along his abs. "You're so gorgeous," I murmured, filled with wonder that he wanted to be here with me.

"And you're fucking perfect," he replied. My head was shaking before I even realized it. "Faith, it's true. You don't see yourself the way everyone else does, but you're beautiful."

My hand moved to the scars that were covered

by the camisole I still wore. The ones no guy had ever seen. The dark red slashes across my skin were the main reason I was so worried about Dillon seeing me naked, even though I knew he had scars of his own. Mine were still so ugly. I loved how he looked at me, and I didn't want to change the way he saw me.

Be brave, I told myself as I slid my fingers lower and tugged him closer by hooking a finger in the waistband of his shorts. I let myself fall backwards onto the soft pile carpet, pulling Dillon with me so his body pressed against mine. Then I wrapped my arms around him. Dillon must have sensed my concern because he hugged me tightly to his body as he spoke.

"You're insanely sexy. It's not just the way you look. There's just something about you that draws me in and I can't look away," he reassured me. "Wanting—no needing—to get closer to you has been driving me crazy ever since we met. I've only managed to hold back because I didn't want to scare you. But don't think, for even one moment, that it's because I don't want you."

"I want you, too," I admitted shyly.

"Only if you're sure," he whispered into my ear, the heat from his breath as he spoke sending shivers up my spine.

This was a big step for me, but I couldn't imagine taking it with anyone other than Dillon. "I'm positive. I want you to make love to me."

"I'll make it so good for you, baby," he murmured against my skin as his lips trailed down my neck.

When his fingers slid up from my waist and tugged on the material of my camisole to lift it over my head, I tensed. Our eyes met after he pulled it off, and I wished with all my heart that we could just keep looking at each other as we made love. His gaze was questioning, and I forced a smile on my face to let him know everything was okay. My desire for him was stronger than my fear, so I tried to let go of my worry as his fingers slid to the back of my bra while he captured my lips for a kiss.

Once it was off, he nibbled and kissed his way down my body. When his body tensed above mine, I knew he had seen my scars. His gaze flew up to mine, and instead of disgust or pity, I saw sadness and pain in his eyes. "The transplant?"

"Yeah, but it's just scar tissue. I'm okay now."

"Better than okay," he corrected. "Perfect."

I didn't realize it at the time, but that was the moment I fell head over heels in love with Dillon. When I was at my most vulnerable, he accepted me exactly as I was. Scars and flaws included.

"Dillon," I sighed as his tongue flicked over one of my nipples while his fingers plucked at the other. When he sucked one deep into his mouth, I felt the pull all the way down to my pussy and my back arched off the floor.

"My tough girl likes that, huh?" he murmured against my breast, his eyes burning into mine as he looked up at me.

"Yes," I hissed out as his mouth moved to the other nipple, biting down gently and then licking the sting away. His hands pressed me against the floor as his lips moved down my stomach, stopping to kiss the scars on both sides of my body. As his tongue traced the puckered skin, it was the first time since my surgery that I didn't hate knowing they were there.

When his hands swept farther down to caress my legs, my focus shifted to the goose-bumps that followed the trail of his fingers. I lifted my hips so he could tug my shorts off and when he spread my legs apart afterwards, all my thoughts scattered. As he held my hips so I couldn't move, I felt his breath through my panties. He kissed around the edges, licking the skin where my upper thighs met my pelvis. I was so drenched that I could feel moisture dripping from me. I jerked against his hold when his finger traced over my pussy, finding the dampness through my panties.

"Lift up, baby," he instructed as he tugged them down my legs.

"Oh my God!" I gasped when his fingers spread me open, and he flicked his tongue over my clit. My body nearly shattered at the feel of his warm mouth on me.

"You're dripping wet for me," he whispered, his breath hot against my pussy before he swept his tongue across my damp flesh.

"So amazing," I moaned.

"Ready for more?"

"Yes."

As soon as I answered, one of his fingers pressed against my opening and slowly slid inside. My legs instinctively widened farther, and I threw my head back against the pillows and moaned.

"Tight," he groaned as he stopped the progress of his finger and didn't move any deeper.

Although I felt stretched at his invasion, it still felt so damn good. "Please don't stop," I begged.

His dark chuckle probably should have scared me, but it just added to my excitement. I watched as he lowered his head and his tongue flicked out to stroke my clit. Clenching his hair in my hands, I drew him closer in the hope that he would never stop. When he slid his finger out and buried his tongue deep inside me, it drove me out of my mind with need.

I was writhing on the floor beneath him, my legs clenching as an orgasm started to build. The first one that I wouldn't give myself. I whimpered when he pulled his tongue from my body, but then he replaced it with his finger again. This time it slid more easily inside and my body started to shudder when he twisted it around and rubbed my G-spot. Then he licked my clit and my trembling increased. When he sucked it hard into his mouth, I felt like a tidal wave came crashing down over my body as my orgasm hit.

"Dillon!" I screamed his name hoarsely, my hips bucking of their own accord and my nails digging into his scalp.

"Mm," he hummed, and the vibrations against my skin sparked another mini-orgasm.

When he finally pulled away from my body, I was covered in a fine sheen of sweat and I was so relaxed I felt like a limp noodle. Dillon kissed his way back up my body and as he held himself above me, I could see some of my wetness still coating his chin. He licked his lips and then kissed me, and I could taste myself on him.

"So fucking perfect," he groaned. "Don't move an inch."

I heard the rustle of his shorts as he kicked them off, and I turned my head to see him kneeling completely naked in front of me. His dick jutted from his body, hard and long. It was so big that I wasn't sure it would fit inside my body. I gulped at the thought of the pain I would probably feel as he reached over to retrieve a condom from his shorts.

"You drive me so crazy, I almost forgot this," he murmured before he ripped the foil package open and rolled it onto his hardened length. When he was done and his eyes met mine again, his expression softened as he took in my fearful look. "There's nothing to be scared of, baby."

"Are you sure it'll fit?" I asked.

Although the question had slipped out when I didn't mean to say it, it seemed like a valid concern until he started laughing. "Yes, Faith. I'll fit inside you because you were made for me."

With those words, the anger which had started to build because of his laughter faded. The idea that this amazing guy thought I was made for him was enough to make my heart melt and to give me the courage I needed to go through with this.

"Then I guess you'd better show me, huh?" I

replied, opening my legs to make room for him as he crawled between them.

"I guess so," he said, his eyes smiling down at me as he pressed the tip of his hard-on against my opening. When he inched inside, his gaze turned serious.

"Now," I whispered.

"Tell me if it hurts too much," he instructed right before he thrust deep, tearing through the proof of my virginity and not stopping until he was deep inside my body.

My eyes slammed shut at the stabbing pain and tears slid down my cheeks. It took me a moment to breathe through the burn until it passed and by then, Dillon started to pull out. "I'm okay," I reassured him, sliding my hands down his back—after I removed my nails from his skin since I'd dug them in without even realizing it.

"Fuck, baby," he groaned. "I'm so sorry."

"It's okay, honey. It had to be done."

He buried his head against my neck and mumbled against my skin. "Seeing you in pain is not okay with me."

"Look at me," I ordered and waited until he lifted his head and his eyes locked with mine. "Do I look like I'm in pain anymore?"

A slight sting was still there, but the arousal I

had felt earlier was building again as I adjusted to the sensation of having him inside me. Seeing the doubt in his eyes, I wiggled my hips experimentally and felt my pussy flutter against him as the movement sent him deeper. I locked my legs around his hips and circled my own, and the answering wetness made his invasion even easier. As he felt the moisture from my body, he finally relaxed.

"No, baby. You don't look like you're in pain anymore," he rasped before pulling out slowly and inching his way back inside. "And you feel fucking perfect. Just like I knew you would."

I lifted my hips, trying to get him to move a little faster. "Dillon," I moaned.

"Gonna make it so good for you," he promised. "And make you forget about the pain."

He pulled out and plunged back in on a hard stroke that drove my body into the floor. I gripped the taut skin of his back and held on as he picked up speed. Without realizing what I was doing, I raked my nails down his back as he continued to thrust into me. As waves of pleasure rolled over my body, my eyes drifted shut.

"I'm so close," I moaned, my body starting to shake again.

Dillon's hips began to thrust faster as he drove himself in and out of my body. I felt like I was suspended on a razor's edge as my pussy clenched against his cock. He leaned down until his lips hovered over my ear.

"Come for me now," he whispered on a puff of hot air as his finger found my clit. The combination of his cock deep inside me, his lips on my ear, and his finger teasing my clit sent me over the edge, and I convulsed around him. He gentled his strokes and stiffened when his own orgasm washed through him. His cock throbbed deep inside me, and I felt the heat of his semen as it spurted into the condom.

When my body went limp under his, he rolled onto the carpet beside me and pulled me into his arms. "Even more perfect than I thought it would be," he murmured against the top of my head.

"Yeah."

"You okay?" He squeezed my body tightly.

"I'm perfect." Really, truly perfect.

It wasn't until he chuckled that I realized I'd borrowed his word. "I'm glad you finally agree with me."

"Just so long as you don't think it's going to happen all the time," I joked, my lips curving into a smile as I cuddled against him. I'd never felt closer to another person in all my life, and it scared me a little to know the power he held over me now.

Chapter Fifteen

FAITH

Almost two months later, I sat across Sarah's desk from her while she stared at me with narrowed hazel eyes, her head tilted to the side. "There's something different about you."

"Different good? Or different bad?"

"Definitely good." She tapped her index finger against her chin. "It's been four years since your transplant, and you look really healthy. How was your most recent round of blood work?"

"The results from November were great, but I haven't seen the report from the lab for the last draw. It was just at the end of last week, so I should get those numbers back soon."

"Are you getting more rest? Drinking more water?" She leaned forward a little, her gaze scanning my face. "Whatever you're doing is really working for you."

I'd just taken a sip of water, and I almost spewed it right in her face because what I'd been doing was Dillon. A lot. Like all of the time. Once we'd had sex that first time on Christmas Eve night, we hadn't been able to keep our hands—and other, more interesting parts of our bodies—off each other.

My cheeks filled with heat, and Sarah's eyes widened. "Is that a blush I see on your face?"

"Um," I mumbled, my blush getting worse. "Maybe?"

"And is it caused by a boy?"

Shit. I hadn't been able to keep it from her for even five minutes into our conversation. Not that I wasn't planning to tell Sarah about Dillon, but I'd thought I'd bring him up at the end of my visit. After we'd gotten past all the important life stuff we needed to discuss because I was only three months away from graduation. "Yeah," I admitted softly.

"Someone special?"

I grinned at her. "Dillon's definitely special."

"Dillon? How did you guys meet? And when? I can't believe so much has changed since I saw you last."

"Remember when I told you about Elaine Montgomery?"

"Of course I remember! How could I forget the woman who's made such an impact on all of your lives?" She leaned back in her chair, shaking her head. "I still can't believe how much she's done for you guys."

"Well," I drawled, chuckling to myself a little. "What she's done for me is a little different than everyone else."

"Really?" She set her elbow on her desk and rested her chin on her palm. "How so?"

"I met Dillon through her." I took a deep breath, trying to settle my nerves. I wasn't sure why I was so nervous to explain their connection unless it was just that I wasn't used to talking about my dating life since I'd never had one before. "Because he's her son."

"Whoa. How'd that happen?" Her voice dropped to a whisper and she leaned so far forward that her chin slipped from her palm. She fell over, her face coming only a couple of inches from smacking against her desk.

"Through his mom." Dillon's secrets were his own to share, so I kept my answer vague. "I totally missed the signs that she was trying to find reasons for us to meet until Dillon pointed her matchmaking attempts out to me at Thanksgiving."

"Thanksgiving, huh? You guys are serious enough that you're spending holidays together?"

"Not back then. Not really." I shook my head. "We'd only been on one actual date, and Elaine was the one who invited me."

"But it's serious now?"

"Yeah, it is. Dillon opened up to me about a lot of stuff at Thanksgiving, and it was kind of a turning point for us." I traced a circle on the top of her desk with a finger. "I guess you could say that's when we officially became a couple."

"Oh, wow," she breathed. "You really like this boy, don't you?"

"I do. I really do." My lips tilted up in a goofy grin. I couldn't stop it, and I didn't even care if it made me look like an idiot. Because I was happy. Being with Dillon made me happy.

"If he makes you smile like that, then I approve. Big time."

"Thanks." I felt my grin getting even goofier, but it only made Sarah offer me a big smile of her own.

"I'm happy for you, Faith. You've faced so much adversity, and yet you still managed to come so far from the girl I met all those years ago." Her eyes filled with tears and she sniffled. "In three months, you're going to be a college graduate." Another sniffle. "With a promising career in social work ahead of you." One lone tear slid down her cheek. "Where you're going to continue the amazing work you've already started doing, with whatever job you take." She reached for a tissue to wipe her eyes and blow her nose. "And you've got a serious boyfriend! Someone you've clearly let inside your heart, judging by the dreamy look on your face any time you mention his name. I'm so, so proud of you."

"Why do I feel like me having a boyfriend is the part you're proudest about?"

A startled laugh burst from her throat. "Because it is?"

"Sarah!" I couldn't believe she'd said that.

"Stop! You know I didn't mean it that way." Her expression turned serious. "It's just that I didn't have any worries about you when it came to college or a career. Not since the day you agreed to apply. Once the decision was made, I knew you'd succeed because you're smart and driven."

"Sarah." I was so moved by what she'd said I could barely speak. Her name was just a whisper of sound that time. I'd felt like she'd believed in me, but to hear her put it that way was just…wow. "Thank you."

"You're welcome." She gave me a watery smile. "Thank you for letting me remain a part of your journey these past few years. Watching what you've accomplished with your second chance has been an honor."

"You're the one who set me on this path," I reminded her. "I would've been working a dead-end job with only a high school diploma if it hadn't have been for you."

Sarah shook her head. "I might've given you the nudge you needed, but you took it and more than ran with it all on your own. You're on course to graduate with honors, and you've got all those other foster kids coming up behind you and following in your footsteps. Because you inspire them, like you inspire me, to be a better person each and every day."

Shit. Now I was the one crying. Sarah was one of the best people I knew. To know she found me inspiring was almost more than my heart could handle. "That inspiration runs both ways, Sarah. You're the reason I picked social work for my major. Because I wanted to follow in your footsteps."

"Oh my God, Faith. I can't even tell you what it means to me, to hear you say that," she cried, reaching across her desk to squeeze my hand.

"It's the truth," I sniffled.

We sat there like that for a couple of minutes before she yanked a few tissues from the box and passed them to me before grabbing some for herself.

"You know what I wish?" she asked.

"What?"

"That I could thank your kidney donor and their family for giving you the second chance you needed. To be able to tell them about the difference you've made in so many lives."

My eyes filled with tears again and they spilled out, trailing down my cheeks. Thinking about my donor and what their family had lost sent me back to that time when I'd thought I was going to die. I hadn't even really known what I would've missed out on back then. Not until I met Dillon and opened myself up to love. Because that's what it was with him...love. Neither of us had used that particular four-letter word yet, but it didn't make the feelings any less real or true. Just unspoken. And the only reason I got to experience love was because someone gave me the gift of life in the depths of their own despair.

"Hey." Sarah tapped on my hand, and it pulled me out of the past and back into the present. "You okay?"

"Yeah, I am." I nodded and offered her a watery smile. "Or I will be."

Once we pulled ourselves together, the conversation turned to graduation and my plans for the future—which I hadn't figured out yet. I was focused on finishing up my classes and making it to graduation...and my relationship with Dillon. But the future was barreling towards me, and I was going to have to decide what I wanted to do soon.

Chapter Sixteen

FAITH

I still hadn't figured out what I was going to do two months later. I'd been waiting to see if the option my heart was set on was going to be a possibility or not. Reading through the letter I'd finally received from the school, I hardly believed my eyes as I sat down on my mattress. "Holy shit."

"Was that a good holy shit or more of an oh-fuck holy shit?" Christine swiveled around on the chair at her desk to stare at me.

"I think it was a little of both."

She rolled across the floor and snatched the paper out of my hands. After scanning the first line, she jumped to her feet and screamed, "Holy shit! You got accepted?"

"I did."

"Of course you did!" She tugged me to my feet, and we danced around the room. "With your grades and that personal statement you wrote; they would have been insane to turn you down. You're going to be the best Master's in Social Work student this school has ever had."

I didn't need an advanced degree to get a job since I could begin working as a social worker with a bachelor's degree. But earning a master's degree meant that I'd achieve the highest level of education for a social worker in Florida. I'd also be eligible for any job in my field after I completed three years of field experience.

"Am I crazy for wanting to stay in school for two more years? Shouldn't I be ready to get a job and enter the real world?"

"Fuck no, you're not crazy." She nudged me towards the bed and sat on the mattress at my side. "It's not like you're running off to join the circus."

"The circus?" I echoed. "Can people run off to join the circus anymore?"

She threw her hands up in the air and shrugged. "I have no idea. It was the best I could come up with the spur of the moment."

"Have you ever even been to the circus?" I laughed. "Talk about totally random."

"What can I say? I'm the queen of random."

She really was good at blurting out completely random stuff at the oddest times, so the circus reference shouldn't have surprised me too much. But I still didn't get her point. "Just because I'm not doing something ridiculous like running off to the circus, doesn't mean I'm not crazy."

"No, but thinking you haven't spent your whole life in the real world means you might be," she pointed out. "You and I? We were born into the real world, and we didn't escape it until we came to college. If you want to spend two more years here, then I say do it. Get your motherfucking master's degree before you get a job. If anyone's earned a reprieve from adulting, it's you."

"And you." I wasn't the only one in the room who'd had a hard life.

"But this isn't about me right now. My path is already determined. We're talking about you and the decision you need to make. Tell me, Faith. What do you want to do?"

I didn't need to think about my answer. I knew what it was. "I want to stay at Southeastern and get my master's degree."

"Then that's what you're going to do."

"There you go." She patted me on the knee. "Decision made."

"Now I just have to tell Dillon."

"Faith?" She dragged my name out to about three syllables. "He knows you applied for grad school, right?"

"Yes, geesh! I'm not that bad."

She crossed her arms over her chest and stared at me with one brow lifted. "But?"

"But I might have mentioned it more in passing. I didn't make a big deal about it because I was afraid to jinx my application. Like talking about it with him would make it too real or something."

"Fuck being worried about shit like that anymore." She wrapped her hands around my upper arms and shook me a little. "You're only a couple of weeks away from graduating with honors. You got your acceptance letter to grad school. And you've got an amazing boyfriend who's crazy in love with you. Live in the moment! Enjoy the amazing life you're building and stop waiting for the other shoe to drop."

She was right. My life was pretty damn amazing. I needed to worry less and enjoy it more. "Do you really think Dillon loves me?"

"Oh my God!" She shook me again. "Have you guys still not told each other yet? You're killing me here, smalls. Pull up your big girl panties and throw it out there."

Ever since I'd put a name to what I was feeling

for Dillon while I'd been sitting in Sarah's office, I'd come so close to saying those three little words to him. But there was a different four-letter word that kept holding me back. Fear. "What if he doesn't say it back?"

"You're barely going to be able to get the words out before he tosses you over his shoulder and *shows* you how exactly how much he loves you."

"Are you sure?"

"Beyond a shadow of a doubt. Pinkie swear." She let go of my arms and lifted one hand up with her pinkie finger sticking out so we could shake them. "If I'm wrong, I promise to run off to the circus with you."

"You're ridiculous," I laughed, shaking my head.

"I am, and that's never going to change." She picked the letter up off the mattress and shoved it in my hand. "But it's time for you to stop being ridiculous and go give your hottie the big news. All of it."

She practically shoved me out the door and dragged me down to where her junker was parked in the lot next to our dorm. Before I knew it, she'd driven me over to Dillon's place and I was standing in front of his door. When it opened, she honked her horn and gave me the thumbs up sign.

"Hey, baby." Dillon leaned down and pressed a kiss against my lips, giving Christine a wave before pulling me inside the house. "I didn't realize you were coming over so early. I thought we were meeting up later tonight. Didn't you need to finish that term paper and get it turned in?"

"Yeah. It was easier than I expected, so it didn't take as long as I thought it would. I emailed it to my professor about thirty minutes ago." I followed him into the living room, running my fingers along the edge of the envelope in the pocket of my shorts.

"You want to do anything special tonight, now that we have more time?" He dropped down onto the couch and pulled me onto his lap, nuzzling against my neck. "Or are you still cool with binge watching a show and eating takeout?"

"It sounds perfect to me. My brain literally feels like it's dead."

"With all the studying you've been doing lately, I'm not surprised. You need to relax, and I'm looking forward to helping you out with that." I shifted on his lap, turning around to straddle him. "You've got that serious look in your eyes. Everything okay?"

"Yeah." I nodded, fiddling with a lock of hair that'd fallen onto his forehead and smoothing it back. "But there's something I need to talk to you about."

I felt his body tense beneath mine, and his hands tightened on my hips. "We need to talk is usually code for bad news."

"This isn't bad," I reassured him as I relaxed in his hold. Christine was right. Dillon was as crazy about me as I was him. I didn't need to be worried about how he'd react when I pulled up my big girl panties and told him how I felt. But that didn't mean I was dying to do it, so I decided to give him my big news first. "Remember when I mentioned that I was applying to grad school?"

"Yeah. Of course I do. When you talk, I listen. Always."

I couldn't help myself. I pressed my lips against his for a kiss because he somehow always knew exactly what to say to make me feel better. "Which is why you're so damn perfect for me and shouldn't worry when I say we need to talk."

"I can't make any promises, baby. You're too important for me to ever take you for granted. If you come to me looking worried and saying we need to talk, then I'm going to be concerned."

"Well, this isn't one of those times when you need to be concerned. I have good news." I pulled the envelope out of my pocket and handed it to him. “Or at least I think it is, and I hope you do too.”

He pulled the letter out, skimming it quickly before his head jerked up and he grinned at me. “You got in?”

“Yup. It looks like I’m going to be a grad student.”

“That’s fantastic, baby. I’m so proud of you!” He brushed his lips against mine and gave the bottom one a little nip with his teeth. “You’re going to kick grad school’s ass, just like you did undergrad.”

“It’s not going to be easy,” I warned him. “The tuition waiver program will cover me for grad school, but the stipend I get for living expenses only lasts until I’m twenty-three. I’m either going to have to take an accelerated course load to try to finish in two semesters plus the summer, or I’m going to have to juggle a job and my classes the second year. But either way, I’m not going to have as much time for you as I do now.”

“And I’m going to be working full-time for my dad. I’m sure my schedule will suck, which is only going to make things more difficult,” he groaned, dropping his head against my shoulder.

“It might be hard, but we’ll figure it out.” We had to because I refused to think otherwise.

His head jerked up and he searched my face with dark eyes. "I might have a solution to our problem."

"Oh, yeah? What is it?"

"Move in with me."

Chapter Seventeen

DILLON

She reared back and looked at me with her pretty brown eyes wide and full of shock. "What?"

"Move in with me," I repeated with conviction. I'd been thinking about asking her since Corey first mentioned it, but the time never seemed right. Until now; when she'd handed me the perfect opportunity.

But judging by the way she was shaking her head, she didn't seem to agree. "While I appreciate the offer, we can't just move in together because it'll fix a problem. Moving in together is huge."

"This isn't a spur of the moment decision on my part. I've been thinking about it since Christmas," I admitted. "I almost gave you a key then, but I figured it was too soon."

"Definitely too soon. I absolutely would've freaked out because I hadn't realized I loved you yet." Her hand came up and pressed against her lips, and her eyes grew even wider. "I didn't mean to say it quite like that."

"But you do love me?"

She nodded jerkily, and her body tightened up under my hands. My brain was still trying to catch up to her admission, and it took me a moment to realize why she was tense. She'd said the words, but I hadn't. "I love you, Faith. So fucking much I can barely stand being apart from you some days."

The tension melted from her body, and her eyes lit with pure, unadulterated joy. "Really?"

"Without question."

"Wow."

"Can I assume your wow means that since we love each other, there's no reason for us not to move in together?"

She grinned at me and nodded. "Yeah, that's what it means."

"Thank fuck."

I yanked her body closer to mine, eliminating the small amount of space between us as I kissed her roughly. My lips were smashed against hers, and

I gripped her hair in one hand while I palmed her ass with the other as I lost myself in her body. When I tore my lips from hers, we were both panting for air.

"You have way too many clothes on."

"We both do," she agreed. She rolled off my lap, and we ripped our shirts over our heads, kicked off our shoes, and pulled our pants down our legs. I'd gone commando, so I was already buck naked when Faith was down to her bra and panties.

I pulled her back onto my lap and traced my fingertips along the edges of her bra cups before palming her tits. She pressed into my hold while she reached around and unclasped her bra. I groaned when I pulled my hands away, and the lacy material fell onto my lap. "You're so fucking gorgeous."

"And all yours," she whispered as she rose up on her knees and wiggled out of her panties.

"Because you love me," I rasped out, needing to hear it again.

"I do. I love you, Dillon."

Her saying it so freely lit a fire inside me. I ran my hands down her spine and gripped her ass, grinding up against her. "Oh, damn," I groaned. "You're so fucking wet. I can't wait to get inside you."

She pressed closer to me. "Don't wait. Take me now."

"I need a taste of you first." I flipped our positions so she was sitting on the couch, and I dropped to my knees on the floor in front of her. I ran my palms along her bare skin, from her ankles to the inside of her upper thighs, and pulled her legs apart. "After I get it, I'll fuck deep inside you until we both can't take any more."

"Yes," she hissed as I licked the outside of her pussy lips. My hands gripped her thighs to hold them open as she clenched them together at my touch.

"Keep 'em open, baby, if you want my mouth on you."

"I do," she whispered, running her fingers through my hair to grip my skull.

I chuckled against her skin, making her tremble before I circled my tongue around her clit without quite touching it. Levering my shoulders between her legs, I jerked her hips up so she was opened wide to me. Snaking my tongue out, I licked up her wet slit.

"I love how you taste," I whispered before sucking her clit into my mouth and flicking it with my tongue several times. Then I released it with a pop and dipped my tongue lower to fuck her pussy with it.

"Yes! Just like that, Dillon," she gasped.

I kept at her until she was writhing beneath me, her body tight as she begged me to let her come. My cock was throbbing at that point, so I pulled my tongue out of her pussy and went after her clit until she flew over the edge. Then I rose up on my knees and positioned myself between her legs.

"Fuck, I need to grab a condom," I groaned as I rubbed the tip of my cock along her pussy lips. We'd talked about going bare, but it wasn't an option for us. Because of the drugs she was on for her transplant, the only pill her doctor was willing to put her on had a higher rate of failure and we were nowhere close to ready to even think about having a baby—especially since it would be more complicated with Faith's health issues. So condoms were a necessity for us.

"Hurry," she urged, her hips lifting as she slid against me, leaving a trail of moisture on my cock.

"Goddammit," I hissed as I pulled away from her to find my shorts. Yanking my wallet out of the pocket, I found a condom and got it on my dick in record speed. Then I lined our bodies back up so that I was between her legs with my cock at her opening again.

"I need you," she whispered, pulling my head down for a kiss.

"Faith," I growled against her lips as I sank into her pussy. Each and every time with her felt so damn good, but this was different. Better. Fucking amazing. "Holy fuck, I love you so fucking much."

"I love you, too. But I'd like to feel you fucking me instead of hearing you say it." She dug her fingernails into my ass and tried to pull me deeper inside.

"Fuck, baby." It slipped out without me realizing what I'd said until she giggled and I felt it around my cock.

"Less talk. More action," she ordered on a laugh.

"Be careful what you wish for, because I'm gonna give it to you," I warned a split-second before I pulled out and thrust back into her all the way. Deep and forceful. Over and over, I pounded into her. So hard the couch started to slide across the floor. Inch by inch. Thrust by thrust until my control hung by a thread, Faith writhing underneath me with her nails digging into my ass. Meeting me for each drive of my hips.

"So close," she begged. "Need it, Dillon. Please."

Desperate to send us both over the edge, I

slipped one hand between us and pinched her clit. I felt her tighten around me as she screamed out my name. Her pussy walls clenched around my cock like a vise, and it was over for me too. My balls drew up and tightened, and fire licked through my veins as my climax roared through me. Planting myself deep, my come filled the condom as my cock jerked over and over again. "Fuck."

"Damn straight," she laughed softly.

"Oh, now you don't mind if I say it?"

"Hell yeah, you fucked me silly." She brushed my hair back from my forehead and pressed a kiss to my lips. "You can say anything you'd like."

It didn't take me more than a second to think of my response. "I love you."

She grinned up at me. Her eyes were a little dazed, her cheeks were flushed, and her lips were swollen. She'd never looked more gorgeous. "Feel free to say that as often as you'd like."

"Be prepared to hear it morning, noon, and night now that you're moving in with me," I warned as I pulled out of her and rose to my feet to pad across the room and toss the condom into the garbage can in the bathroom off the living room. Then I splashed my face with water and washed my hands before wandering towards the kitchen to grab us a couple of bottles of water.

Faith was still on the couch, but she'd slipped my shirt on, when I walked back into the living room and handed her one of the bottles. "You better hydrate because that wasn't our only round for the night."

"Oh really?" She quirked an eyebrow at me.

"You told me you love me and you're going to move in with me." I flashed her a grin. "We need to celebrate. Repeatedly."

"I guess I'm okay with the change in plan." Her exaggerated sigh turned into a giggle when I dropped down next to her and dug my fingers into her sides. "Stop! Okay! I guess we can binge on sex instead of shows, but I still want that takeout food because I'm starving."

"I'll get extra. All your favorites," I promised, pulling up an app on my phone to place an order for delivery. "And while we're waiting for it to get here, you can make a plan to get you moved in here. When were you thinking?

"After graduation maybe?"

That was only two weeks away, but it was about thirteen days longer than I wanted to wait. "How about tomorrow?"

"Tomorrow? No way." She shook her head. "I have exams to study for still. I don't have time to pack up my dorm room. Not yet. It's going to have to wait until after finals at the very least. Maybe right after graduation would work best?"

I claimed her lips in a hard kiss to stop her litany of reasons for why she couldn't move in right away. "No backpedaling, baby. You're moving in. Period. End of story. I'm willing to wait until after graduation if I have to, but only if you spend your nights here."

"Will you keep feeding me my favorite foods and giving me lots of orgasms?"

"Of fucking course."

"Then I guess I can agree to that deal."

That was a good thing because if her answer had been no, I would've had to hire a mover as a surprise and then fuck her until she didn't want to argue about it anymore.

Chapter Eighteen

FAITH

A little more than a week later, my last undergrad exam was finally over. I only had graduation left to get through, and I found myself with some alone time. Dillon was at his dad's office. Christine was taking her last final. And I was packing up another box of stuff to bring over to Dillon's place.

Or our place, actually, since I'd been slowly moving in with him. Most of my clothes were already there, and I was grabbing some of my random stuff today. Practically living with him was easier than I expected, and it made me worry less about how things were going to work after graduation.

Living together meant truly opening ourselves

up. No keeping parts of ourselves hidden. Like when you have guests coming over and you didn't want them to see all your shit. Instead of going through it all to clean it up, you shove it in a drawer to hide it away. That only worked with guests, though. Which meant I needed to really clean my shit up instead of just hiding it away...starting with that conversation I'd had with Sarah about thanking my donor's family for the second chance they'd given me. I never would have had the happiness I'd found with Dillon without them. It didn't seem right to move on to the next phase of our lives together without acknowledging their sacrifice in some way.

Pulling my phone out of my pocket, I dialed the number for Dr. Stewart's physician's assistant, Lisa. One of the advantages of being a patient there for several years was easier access when you had a question.

"Hey, Faith. Everything okay? We don't have you down for your next appointment for another two and a half months. Did you need to come in sooner?"

I'd learned early on that Lisa was the kind of person whose mouth moved a hundred miles per minute, so you had to be quick if you wanted to get a word in edgewise. "No, I'm good. I was just wondering if it's possible for me to reach out to my donor's family. To say thank you."

"There are rules against us disclosing their contact information."

Disappointment crashed down on me. "Oh."

"But you can write a letter, care of the transplant center. We'll forward it to them for you."

"Oh!" That time it was said in relief. "That would be amazing. So I just write the letter, drop it off to you guys, and you'll take care of everything else for me?"

"Pretty much, yes. But you'll want to make sure to not include your last name or where you live. The state is fine, just not the city. And it goes without saying, no contact information."

"Great! I'd prefer not to wait until my next appointment, so I'll probably stop in sometime this week with a letter."

"We'll see you then."

Determined to move forward into my future with Dillon surrounded by positivity, I sat down to write my letter. Finding the right words to use was one of the most difficult things I'd ever done. By the time I was satisfied, I had rewritten it about a dozen times.

Dear Donor Family,

I received the precious gift of a donated kidney from your loved one. There are no words that can truly express the depth of gratitude I feel towards your family. It takes a special kind of person to make such a sacrifice in their time of grief and need. I will never be able to thank you enough for giving me a second chance at life, but you have my promise that I have tried to live up to the example set by your loved one. And I'll continue to do so.

I'm sorry it has taken me so long to write this letter. My life was drastically different four years ago when I received my transplant. I was a senior in high school who felt like there wasn't anything good to look forward to, even though I was willing to fight to live. My childhood was difficult, and I wasn't raised with the best role models surrounding me. Your family's decision was the first genuine act of sacrifice I ever experienced. It's one I value more than I can ever explain. Your loved one didn't just save my life, they gave me a whole new outlook on the world by giving me the very thing I was named after—faith.

Thanks to the second chance your family gave me, I have so many positive things in my life now. I'm graduating with honors from college soon, with a bachelor's degree in social work. I've been accepted into a graduate program and plan to go on to earn my master's.

While in school, I met a boy and fell in love for the first time in my life. We're in the process of moving in together. I'm living a blessed life I never expected to have because of your loved one.

I know your decision to donate their organs must have been incredibly difficult, but I wanted you to know what a difference it has made in my life. I will never be able to fully express my gratitude to you for giving me this opportunity. I hope this letter brings you a little solace in knowing some good came out of your loss. Thank you for making the decision to save my life.

With inexpressible gratitude,
Faith

I started sobbing when I finished reading through the final version. Tears were streaming down my face as I tucked it into an envelope and put it in my purse. A quick glance at my phone showed that I still had an hour left before Dillon would be home, so I decided to grab a rideshare to the doctor's office to drop it off. The driver kept sneaking glances at me through the rearview mirror. I was sure he thought there was something horribly wrong with me when he agreed to wait the five minutes I told him it would take before I came back out.

I took the stairs up four floors instead of waiting for the elevator. I was out of breath, red-faced, and bleary-eyed when I walked into Dr. Stewart's office. I'd gone in there looking worse in the past, and one of the good things about being in a medical center was that nobody looked at me oddly as I walked up to the receptionist's desk.

"Hey, Faith," Susan greeted me. "Lisa sent me an email about an hour ago letting me know you might stop by sometime this week with a letter for your donor family. But I didn't expect to see you so soon."

"Yeah." I pulled the envelope out of my purse. "Once I had the idea in my head, I couldn't let go of it. I know it's been years, but it suddenly seemed so important. So I thought it would be best to get it done right away."

"That sounds like a smart plan to me." She held out her hand, and I reluctantly passed the letter over. She had to tug on it to get me to let go.

"Sorry, it feels like giving away a part of myself."

"You're putting it in good hands. I'll make sure this gets forwarded as soon as possible," she assured me.

"Thanks." I flashed her an apologetic smile. "How long does that usually take?"

"A week, two at the most."

"And then they'll have it?"

She nodded. "Yes, Faith. You've done the hard part, and I'll do the rest."

"Thank you."

"This is my favorite part of my job, but you're welcome." She beamed a smile at me.

I walked out with a matching grin on my face, feeling like I'd accomplished something good. My smile grew when we pulled up in the driveway and Dillon's car was already there. But my eyes must've still been red-rimmed because as soon as he spotted me walking through the door, he rushed over.

"What happened? Are you okay? Did someone hurt you?" He cupped the sides of my face with his palms and tilted my head back. "You've been crying."

"I swear you have an eagle eye."

"When it comes to you? Damn straight I notice everything." His thumbs swept across my cheeks. "Like your red-rimmed eyes and nose. What the fuck happened? And who the hell do I have to kill for hurting you?"

"Come sit down with me," I urged, taking hold of his hand to lead him over to the couch in the living room. I stroked his arm, trying to calm him down. I was in awe over how he'd leapt into protective mode over me, just because he could tell I'd been crying. "I'm so damn lucky to have you."

"No, baby. You've got that backwards. I'm the lucky one here, and I know it. And I've got no problem putting in the work to prove it to you." He pressed a kiss against my lips. "But I can't do that if you don't tell me what made you cry."

"I made myself cry over a letter I wrote to my donor family." I scrunched up my nose and waited for his reaction because it sounded so ridiculous; me literally making myself cry.

"They let you do that? Communicate with your donor family?"

I explained to him about how the transplant center was going to forward the letter for me, and my reasons behind writing it.

"That's so fucking beautiful, Faith. I'm proud as shit to know I've made you so happy that you wanted to do something like that." He rested his forehead against mine. "Although I should technically kick my own ass for making you cry, even if it was indirectly."

"What if I think you deserve a reward instead?" I closed the inch separating our lips. "For making me ridiculously happy?"

"You aren't going to get any complaints from me." He lifted me up and carried me into the bedroom. "If my woman wants to give me a reward, I'm going to let her."

Lucky for me, my man felt like his reward earned me one in return.

Chapter Nineteen

FAITH

Shopping with Elaine was usually a super fun experience, but it could also be incredibly awkward at times. I was her son's girlfriend. His live-in girlfriend, at that. So when she pulled an insanely cute bra and panty set off the rack to show it to me, I literally almost died of embarrassment.

"Elaine! You can't show me stuff like that," I hissed. "And you certainly can't buy it for me."

"But it's so pretty," she complained when I yanked it out of her hands and put it back on the shelf.

"You can show me all the pretty clothes you want, as long as it's stuff I can wear out in public. No lingerie!"

"If I had your figure, I'd seriously consider wearing that in public."

"You wouldn't," I muttered. "You really, really wouldn't."

"If you knew me back when I was your age," she laughed, shaking her head. "Let's just say, you might be shocked."

"Okie dokie. I think this shopping trip is over. I shouldn't have let you get that last glass of wine with lunch."

"Maybe you're right," she sighed as I led her through the store and out the door to the parking lot where we'd left her car about five hours earlier. "I'm terrible at day drinking nowadays. I used to be able to polish off a bottle of wine with my friends over lunch. Easy peasy. But look at me now. I had two glasses with a full meal hours ago, and I'm going to have to give you the keys because there's no way I can drive home."

"Lucky for both of us, you don't have to physically hand them over," I muttered as I helped her into the car. I was thankful for the technology behind proximity keys after she'd searched her insanely large purse for several minutes without being able to find them. Those two glasses of wine really must have done a number on Elaine, because she fell asleep less than five minutes from the mall.

She didn't wake up when I pulled into the attached garage and turned off the engine.

"C'mon, let's get you inside so you can get more comfortable for your nap." I helped her out of the car, into the house, and onto one of the couches in the family room.

"Can you grab the mail for me?" she asked after I spread a throw blanket over her.

"Sure, let me bring the shopping bags in first."

"Leave your stuff in the trunk and drive the car home. I'll have Lloyd bring me over later so we can pick it up." She gave a sleepy yawn and cuddled into the cushions.

Driving back to her house with Elaine in the passenger seat was one thing. Taking her car out by myself was a completely different story. "I can't, Elaine. It's worth more than I'll make in like ten years as a social worker. What if something happened? I'll just get a rideshare. It's easier."

"No." She reached out and grabbed my hand. "It's just a car, no matter how much Lloyd and I paid for it. Dillon hates when you use a rideshare. That's why he talked you into getting your driver's license. So you wouldn't have to do that anymore."

She was right. It did drive Dillon crazy with worry about what could happen to me with strangers driving me around. It was how he'd finally gotten me to agree to go car shopping with him this weekend. He'd insisted I needed my own set of wheels because I was always so weird about driving his since it was also crazy expensive. At least I'd gotten him to agree to letting me set limits on what kind of car he could buy me.

"Fine," I huffed. "But it's going to take me forever to get home because I'm going to go about five miles under the speed limit the entire way."

"As long as you get there safe and sound, that's all that matters." I pressed a soft kiss to her cheek, and she gave my hand a squeeze. "Could you check the mail on your way out? If there's anything in there, just toss it on the passenger seat and I'll get it when we come pick up the car."

"Sure thing." It was the least I could do after she'd treated me to such a fun day.

I grabbed her shopping bags from the trunk of the car and set them on the kitchen counter before driving down to the mailbox. As I pulled the envelopes out and went to toss them on the passenger seat, one dropped onto my lap. When I picked it up, my eyes landed on the return address. The one for the same transplant center where I received care. The same place I'd stopped off at a week and a half ago to drop off the letter they were going to forward to my donor family.

Sitting there frozen, I frantically tried to think of a reason—any reason other than the one which had already popped into my brain—for why they would be getting mail from the transplant center where I'd had my surgery. But I wasn't able to come up with anything other than the one reason that would tear my whole world apart. Dillon's identical twin brother, Declan.

"This doesn't make any sense. The timing was totally off," I mumbled to myself. "The car accident was an entire month before my transplant, and Dillon said his brother died in the crash."

As I started the engine, my hands were shaking. I carefully turned onto the street and drove away. Once I'd driven about a mile, I pulled over and lifted the envelope off my lap. Staring at it, I tried to talk myself out of opening it.

"Don't do this, Faith." I traced my fingers over the back of the envelope where it was sealed. Opening it would be wrong on so many levels. Whatever was inside wasn't meant for my eyes. It was sent to Dillon's parents—not me. But if the contents were what I thought they might be, then I wanted to be the first person who knew.

Not just want. I needed to be.

Before I could think about it too much more, I ripped the envelope open. Unfolding the typed letter on the transplant center's letterhead, my heart dropped when I recognized the note inside. The one I had written to my donor family.

"No," I wailed. "It can't be. Please, no."

The fear that took hold of me was instantaneous. What if Dillon and his parents hated me because of this? What if that pull we'd felt towards each other was because his identical twin's kidney was inside my body? Would he still love me when he found out?

I sat there and cried for at least an hour, utterly destroyed by the contents of that envelope. The past was not an old coat that could be easily discarded and quickly forgotten. It was a scent that clung and never let go. Only it wasn't just my fucked up past that had come back to wrap its stench around me. It was Dillon's, too. And neither of us had ever seen it coming.

Acknowledgments

Fortuity wouldn't have happened without the help of so many people. I owe thanks to LJ Anderson (Mayhem Cover Design) and Sara Eirew Photography for how beautiful the cover turned out. Ellie McLove (Gray Ink) and Manda Lee for their eagle eyes during the editing process. Elle Christensen, Ella Fox, and S Van Horne for their input on the story as it developed. Sarah Ferguson from Social Butterfly PR for all her help in spreading the word. Kathy Snead Williams for holding my hand while also giving me lots of nudges along the way. Becca Hensley Mysoor for her insight during a wonderful lunch. The #DreamTeam and DHI for cheering me on. My Racy Readers for their continued support over the years. Dear friends like Aurora

Rose Reynolds and TM Frazier who're always there for me when I need them. My mom, whose transplant journey provided inspiration. My sons, who put up with all my craziness when I'm writing and continue to cheer me along. I'm sure I'm missing some incredible people because it truly has taken a village to bring this project to life, and I'm blessed to be surrounded by such an amazing village.

Thank you!

Rochelle Paige

Also by Rochelle Paige

BLYTHE COLLEGE SERIES

Push the Envelope

Hit the Wall

Summer Nights (novella duo)

Outside the Box

Winter Wedding (novella)

BACHELORETTE PARTY SERIES

Sucked Into Love

Checked Into Love

CRISIS SERIES

Identity Crisis

FATED MATES SERIES

Black River Pack:

Crying Wolf

Shoot for the Moon

Thrown to the Wolves

McMahon Clan:

Bear the Consequences

Bear It All

Bear the Burden

About the Author

I absolutely adore reading—always have and always will. When I was growing up, my friends used to tease me when I would trail after them, trying to read and walk at the same time. If I have down-time, odds are you will find me reading or writing.

I am the mother of two wonderful sons who have inspired me to chase my dream of being an author. I want them to learn from me that you can live your dream as long as you are willing to work for it.

Connect with me online:

Made in the USA
Las Vegas, NV
08 May 2023

71734426R00135